THUMBELINA
AND OTHER STORIES

To Sarah,
our Sweet Sweet
Niece,

Merry Christmas
With Lots of Love,
Aunt Karen
+
Uncle Bob

12/25/96

THUMBELINA
AND OTHER STORIES

by Hans Christian Andersen

Illustrated by Margaret W. Tarrant

Derrydale Books
New York • Avenel

Published by Derrydale Books, distributed by
Random House Value Publishing, Inc.
40 Engelhard Avenue, Avenel, New Jersey 07001

Random House
New York • Toronto • London • Sydney • Auckland

Designed by Liz Trovato
Edited by Nina Rosenstein
Production supervised by Ellen Reed

Printed and bound in Singapore

Library of Congress Cataloging-in-Publication Data
Andersen, H.C. (Hans Christian), 1805-1875. [Tales. English. Selections.]
Thumbelina & other stories / by Hans Christian Andersen.
p. cm.
Contents: Thumbelina — Nightingale — Little swineherd—Emperor's new clothes
— Little mermaid — Ugly duckling — Princess and the pea.
ISBN 0-517-12215-4
1. Fairy tales—Denmark. 2. Children's stories, Danish—Translations into English. 3. Fairy tales.
I. Title. II. Title: Thumbelina.
PZ8.A54 1995
[Fic]—dc20
94-35478
CIP
AC

8 7 6 5 4 3 2 1

Contents

Introduction 7

Thumbelina 9

The Little Swineherd 27

The Emperor's New Clothes 35

The Nightingale 43

The Ugly Duckling 57

The Princess and the Pea 71

The Little Mermaid 73

Introduction

ALMOST two hundred years ago in Denmark there lived a boy who was very tall and very skinny and spoke in a high-pitched voice. The other schoolchildren teased him and mocked him cruelly, so he was happy only at home, where he could play by himself with his wonderful homemade theatrical stage. He loved to make up stories and act them out using a whole cast of doll-actors.

This little boy was Hans Christian Andersen, a gawky, ugly duckling of a child who grew up into a swan of a storyteller. He wrote many serious novels, travel books, plays, and poems, but he became famous throughout the world for his children's stories. In this book you will find seven of his favorite tales, beautifully illustrated by Margaret W. Tarrant. Some of them may already be your favorites, too.

Andersen got many of the ideas for his stories from his everyday life and what he saw around him. He knew what it was like to be poor and sad and lonely. He also loved nature, and he once said, "Every little flower says, 'Just look at me. Then you'll know my story.'" Perhaps he was looking at a little flower when he dreamed up the story of Thumbelina, a tiny little girl no bigger than a thumb, and all her adventures among the creatures of the woods. As a grown-up he learned how it felt to love someone who doesn't love you back. In "The Little Swineherd," a prince woos a spoiled princess and then teaches her a lesson—maybe Andersen wished he could have done the same to the ladies who rejected his love.

In this book you will also read about the vain Emperor who made quite a spectacle of himself in "The Emperor's New Clothes." You will meet "The Nightingale," whose sweet music enchanted a Chinese Emperor, and the princess in "The Princess and the Pea," who must pass the true test of royalty. Finally, there's "The Little Mermaid," who yearned to explore the world beyond the sea, and "The Ugly Duckling," who, like Hans Christian Andersen himself, wanted nothing more than acceptance and love.

So turn the page and enter the world where Hans Christian Andersen himself was most at home—a world of talking animals and magic happenings, a world of cruelty and kindness, love and adventure. In this world you may find some of your very own hopes and fears and dreams.

Thumbelina

HERE was once a woman who wanted very much to have a child, but had no idea where to find one. So she went to an old witch and said to her, "I do so long to have a little child. Will you tell me where I can get one?"

"We'll soon get over that difficulty," said the witch. "Here is a barleycorn. It is not the kind that grows in the farmer's fields, or that chickens are given to eat. Put in a flowerpot and you'll see something, I promise you."

"Thank you," said the woman. So she gave the witch twelve silver pennies, went home, and planted the barleycorn. Immediately a beautiful flower grew. It looked just like a tulip, but the petals were all folded tightly together as if it were still budding.

"What a pretty flower!" said the woman, and she kissed the lovely red and yellow petals. At that very moment the flower gave a loud crack and opened. It was a real tulip, anyone could see that, but right in the middle sat a tiny little girl. She was only as big as a thumb, so they called her Thumbelina.

The woman made her a splendidly polished walnut shell for her cradle, with blue violet petals for a mattress and a rose petal for her blanket. There she slept at night, but in the daytime she played on the table, where the woman put a plate surrounded by a wreath of flowers with their stems in the water. Thumbelina loved to sail from one

end of the plate to the other on a large tulip petal, using two white horsehairs as oars. It was such a pretty sight. She could sing, too, sweetly and softly.

One night, as Thumbelina lay in her pretty cradle, an ugly old toad came hopping through a broken pane in the window. The toad was big and wet and hopped right onto the table where Thumbelina lay sleeping beneath the red rose petal.

"She would make a very nice wife for my son," said the toad, and with that she picked up the walnut shell in which Thumbelina lay and hopped off through the broken pane out into the garden. A large broad river ran there, but near the bank it was swampy and muddy, and there lived the toad and her son. He, too, was nasty and ugly, like his mother.

"Koax-koax-brekke-ke-kex!" was all he could say when he saw the pretty little girl in the walnut shell.

"Don't chatter so loudly or you'll wake her!" said the old toad. "We'll put her out in the river, on one of the broad water-lily leaves— she is so light and little that it will be like a big island to her. She can't escape from there while we are getting the room under the mud ready for you to live together and keep house."

Out in the river grew many clumps of water lilies with broad green leaves. The leaf that was farthest out was also the largest. The old toad swam out to it and placed Thumbelina, nutshell and all, on top of it.

Poor little Thumbelina awoke quite early in the morning. When she saw where she was, she began to cry bitterly, for there was water on every side of the big green leaf and there was no way she could get ashore.

The old toad was busy down in the mud, decorating Thumbelina's new room with marsh grasses and yellow flowers, for she wished her new daughter-in-law to find it pretty and tidy. When she finished she and her ugly son swam to the leaf where Thumbelina sat. They

wanted to take her pretty bed back to the bridal chamber before the bride herself arrived.

The old toad bowed low in the water and said, "Let me introduce my son. He is to be your husband, and you will live together pleasantly down in the mud."

"Koax-koax-brekke-ke-kex!" was all the toad's ugly son could say for himself.

So they took the pretty little cradle and swam away with it. Thumbelina sat alone on the green leaf and cried. She did not want to live in the nasty toad's house, nor have her ugly son for a husband. The little fishes who were swimming in the water had seen the toad and heard what she said, and they stuck their heads up to see the little girl. When they saw her they thought her so pretty that they were quite angry at the idea of her marrying the ugly toad. No, they agreed, that should never be.

They swam around the green stem of the lily leaf below the water and gnawed through it. Then the leaf drifted away down the river with Thumbelina. It floated far, far away, where the toad could not follow.

As Thumbelina sailed along, the little birds in the bushes looked at her and sang, "What a sweet little girl!" On floated the leaf, farther and farther away, as little Thumbelina continued her travels.

A pretty little white butterfly hovered over her, and at last it settled on the leaf, for it had taken quite a fancy to Thumbelina. She was happy, for now the toad could not get her; and as she sailed along, the sun shone on the water like glistening gold and everything was very pretty. She took off her belt and tied one end of it around the butterfly and the other end to the leaf, so now she glided along more quickly than ever.

Presently a big beetle came flying along. He caught sight of Thumbelina and instantly flew down, put his claw around her dainty waist, and carried her up into a tree. The green leaf continued sailing down

the river and the butterfly with it, for he was fastened to the leaf and could not get away.

How frightened poor little Thumbelina was when the beetle flew up into the tree with her. But she was worried most of all about the poor white butterfly that she had tied to the leaf. If he could not get loose, he would surely starve to death. But the beetle did not trouble himself about that at all. He sat down with Thumbelina on the largest green leaf in the tree, gave her some honey from the flowers to eat, and told her that she was very pretty, although she did not resemble a beetle in the least.

After that the other beetles who lived in the tree came for a visit. They looked at Thumbelina and shook their feelers and said, "Why she has only two legs—what a fright she is!" "She has no feelers at all," they went on. "Just look how slender her waist is. Fie! She looks just like a human being! How ugly she is."

All the lady beetles said this, although Thumbelina was really very pretty. The beetle who had flown off with her thought so too, but since all the others said she was ugly, he at last began to believe she really was so. He would have nothing more to do with her. She could go where she liked, he said.

The beetles flew down from the tree with Thumbelina and placed her on a daisy. She sat there and cried because she was so ugly that even beetles would have nothing to do with her. And yet she was really the loveliest little thing, as fine and delicate as the most beautiful rose petal.

All through the summer poor Thumbelina lived alone in the forest. She wove a canopy of grass stalks and hung it up under a large leaf so the rain could not fall upon her. She gathered honey from the flowers for her food, and drank the dew that lay fresh every morning on the leaves. The summer and the autumn passed quickly. Then winter came, the long, cold winter. All the birds that had sung so prettily flew away, the flowers withered, the trees shed their leaves; the large leaf Thumbelina had lived under shriveled and became a yellow, withered stalk. She felt horribly cold, for her clothes were in rags and she herself was so small and delicate that she would surely freeze to death. Poor little Thumbelina! And then it began to snow, and every snowflake that fell upon her was just like a whole shovelful of snow upon a child, for she was only the size of a thumb. She wrapped herself up in a withered leaf, but it did not warm her at all and she shivered with cold.

Near the forest there was a large cornfield, but the corn had long since been harvested. Only the bare, dry stalks remained on the

frozen ground. Indeed, to Thumbelina it was just like another great forest. Oh, how she shivered as she walked through it! Soon she came to a field mouse's door. It was a little hole right under the dry stalks. Inside lived an old field mouse, quite warm and cozy. She had a whole room full of corn, and a nice kitchen and panty. Poor Thumbelina stood outside the door, like a beggar, and asked for a grain of barley, for she had not had anything to eat for two days.

"You poor little creature," said the field mouse, for she was kindhearted. "Come into my warm room and dine with me!"

Afterward, since she liked Thumbelina, she said, "You are quite welcome to stay with me all winter, but you must keep my room nice and clean and tell me stories, for I am very fond of stories."

Thumbelina agreed and did all that the good old mouse required of her, and had a very pleasant time.

"We shall soon be having a visitor," said the field mouse one day. "My neighbor always visits me once a week. He has a better house than I, for he has vast halls and wears a beautiful black fur coat. If only you could have him for a husband, you would be well provided for. But unfortunately he cannot see. Now mind, tell him the very prettiest stories you know."

But Thumbelina did not give it a thought, for she knew that the neighbor was only a mole. Soon he arrived to pay them a visit, wearing a rich black fur coat. He was very wealthy and educated, said the field mouse, and his house was ten times as large as hers, but he absolutely could not endure the sun and he spoke insultingly of the pretty flowers, since he had never seen them.

The field mouse asked Thumbelina to sing to him, and she sang "Fly Away Beetle!" and "The Blackcap Trips the Meadow Along." The mole fell in love with her because of her sweet voice, but he said nothing at the time, for he was very discreet.

He had recently dug himself a long passage under the earth from his own house to theirs, and he gave the field mouse and Thumbelina

 15

permission to walk through it whenever they liked. At the same time he told them not to be frightened by a dead bird that lay in the tunnel. It was a whole bird, complete with feathers and beak. It must have died quite recently, when the winter began, and had been buried in the mole's passage.

The mole took a piece of decaying wood in his mouth, for it shines like fire in the dark, and went in front to light their way through the long, dark tunnel. When they came to the dead bird, the mole put his broad nose through the earth above and made a large hole. Through this the light shone on the body of a dead swallow, with its pretty wings folded down to its sides, and its head and legs drawn in beneath its feathers. The poor bird had certainly died of cold.

Thumbelina felt very sorry for it. She was fond of all little birds—hadn't they sung and twittered for her so prettily all through the summer? But the mole gave it a kick with his short legs and said, "It will chirp no more now. How miserable it must be to born a little bird. Thank goodness none of my children will be *that!* Birds like that have nothing in the world but their 'Kwee-wit! Kwee-wit!' and must starve to death in the winter, stupid things!"

"You may well say that, sensible creature that you are," remarked the field mouse. "What has a bird to show for itself when the winter comes, for all its 'Kwee-witting'? It must starve and freeze to death!"

Thumbelina said nothing, but when the mole and the field mouse had turned their backs on the dead bird, she bent down over it and kissed its closed eyes. "Perhaps it was this very one that sang so prettily to me in the summer," she thought. "What joy it gave me, the lovely, darling bird!"

The mole now closed up the hole through which the daylight shone and escorted the ladies home. But that night Thumbelina could not sleep, so she got up from her bed, wove a large and pretty rug of hay, and took it down to spread around the dead bird, laying some soft wool, which she had found in the field mouse's room, at the sides of the bird, to warm its bed on the cold earth.

 16

"Farewell, you pretty little bird!" she said. "Farewell, and thank you for your pretty songs in the summertime, when all the trees were green and the sun shone so warmly upon us!"

Then she laid her head on the bird's breast. She was startled, for it was just as if something inside was going "Thump! Thump!" It was the bird's heart. The bird was not really dead: it had been stunned by the cold, and as it warmed up, life began to return. In the autumn the swallows fly away to warmer lands, but if one is late and gets left behind, it gets so cold that it falls down as if dead, and the cold snow comes and buries it.

Thumbelina trembled with fright, for the bird was large, compared with herself. But she plucked up her courage, wrapped the wool more closely around the poor swallow, and brought the leaf she had used as a quilt and placed it over the bird's head.

The next night she again crept down to the swallow. There he was, quite alive, but so weak that he could only open his eyes for a second and look at Thumbelina, who stood there with a little piece of decaying wood in her hand, for she had no other light.

"Many thanks, you pretty little child," said the sick swallow. "I am so nice and warm now. I shall soon get back my strength and be able to fly away into the warm sunshine."

"Oh, not yet!" said Thumbelina. "It is so cold outside—it is snowing and freezing! Stay in your warm bed, and I will look after you!" She brought the swallow some water in a leaf. When it had drunk, it told her how it had torn one of its wings on a thornbush, and therefore could not fly as strongly as the other swallows that were leaving for the warm lands. Then the swallow had fallen to the ground, but he could not remember anything more and did not know how he had gotten there.

The swallow stayed the whole winter, and Thumbelina was kind to him and loved him very much. Neither the mole nor the field mouse was told a word about the swallow, for Thumbelina knew they did not like birds.

As soon as spring came and the sun had warmed the earth, the swallow said good-bye to Thumbelina, who opened the hole that the mole had made in the ground. The sun shone in gloriously, and the swallow asked if she would go with him—she could sit on his back and they would fly far out into the green woods. But Thumbelina knew that the old field mouse would be very sad if she left her like that.

"No, I cannot come," said Thumbelina.

"Good-bye, good-bye, you good, pretty little girl," said the swallow, and he flew out into the warm sunshine. Thumbelina watched

him go and tears came to her eyes, for she dearly loved the swallow.

"Kwee-wit! Kwee-wit!" sang the bird as he flew away into the green woods. Thumbelina was very sorrowful. She was never allowed to go into the warm sunshine. The corn that had been planted in the field over the field mouse's house had grown so tall that it seemed like a thick forest to the poor little girl who was only the size of a thumb.

"This summer you must sew your wedding clothes," said the field mouse, for by this time their neighbor, the tiresome mole, had made up his mind that he wanted her to be his wife. "You must have both linen and wool in your wardrobe, for when you become the mole's bride you must wear only the best."

So Thumbelina had to spin away, and the field

mouse hired four spiders to weave for her night and day. Every evening the mole paid them a visit, and he always talked about the same thing, saying that when summer came to an end the sun would not be so hot. Yes, and when summer was over the wedding with Thumbelina was to take place, but she did not like that at all, for she could not bear the boring mole.

Every morning when the sun arose, and every evening when it set, she sneaked outdoors, and when the wind blew aside the cornstalks, so that she could see the blue sky, she thought how beautiful it was in the light. She longed to see the dear swallow once more. But he never returned—he must certainly have flown far away into the woods.

When autumn came Thumbelina's wedding outfit was ready.

"In four weeks you shall be married," said the field mouse. But Thumbelina began to cry, and said that she could not marry the tiresome mole.

"Fiddlesticks!" said the field mouse. "Don't be obstinate or I shall bite you with my white teeth. Such a handsome husband you're going to have, too! What more do you want? The Queen herself does not have such a magnificent black fur coat. He has lots of food, too, in his kitchen as well as his cellar. Be thankful for such a husband, I say!"

And so Thumbelina and the mole were to be married. He had already come to take Thumbelina away; she was to live with him deep down in the ground, and never come up into the warm sunlight, for he could not bear it. The poor child was so distressed, but she asked permission to say farewell to the sun, for while she had lived with the field mouse she had always been allowed to stand in the doorway and look at the sun.

"Farewell, dear golden sun," she said, and stretched her arms high in the air, even going a little way beyond the field mouse's door, for the corn had been picked and only dry stalks stood in the field now. "Farewell, farewell!" she cried, and threw her tiny arms around a

little scarlet flower growing there. "Greet the dear swallow for me if you ever see him!"

"Kwee-wit! Kwee-wit!" sounded at the very moment high above Thumbelina's head. She looked up. It was the swallow just passing by. As soon as he saw Thumbelina he was delighted. He flew down and landed right next to her. She told him how she disliked the idea of having the nasty mole for a husband, and of having to live with him deep down under the ground, where the sun never shone. She could not keep back her tears.

"The cold winter is coming now," said the swallow. "I am going to fly far away to the warm lands. Will you come with me? You can sit upon my back. Just tie yourself on with your belt, and then we will fly away from the ugly mole and his dark room. We will go right over the mountains to the warm lands where the sun shines lovelier than here, and where it is always summer. Do fly away with me, sweet little Thumbelina, who saved my life when I lay frozen in the dark cellar!"

"Yes, I'll go with you," said Thumbelina happily. She sat on the bird's back, her feet resting on his outspread wings, and tied her belt tight to one of his strongest feathers. The swallow flew high into the air, over forests and over sea, and high up over the big mountains capped with snow. Thumbelina was almost frozen in the cold air, but she crept right in under the bird's warm feathers, peeping out now and then to see all the beautiful things beneath her.

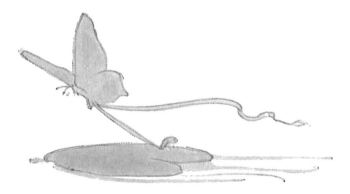

At last they came to the warm lands. There the sun shone much more brightly, the sky was twice as high, and the loveliest green and blue grapes grew everywhere. In the woods lemons and oranges hung on the trees. There was a fragrance of balsam and myrtle, and along the roads ran lovely children playing with large speckled but-

terflies. But the swallow flew still farther, and everything became lovelier and grander. Beneath stately green trees near a blue lake stood a dazzlingly white marble palace from the olden times. Vine tendrils twined up and around the high pillars. At the very top were a number of swallow's nests.

"Here is my house," said the swallow, "but please choose one of the most splendid of the flowers that grow, and I'll put you there and you shall be as happy as you wish."

"Oh, that will be lovely!" she cried, clapping her tiny hands.

On the ground lay a large white marble column that had fallen and broken into three pieces. Between them grew the loveliest white flowers. The swallow flew down with Thumbelina and placed her on one of the broad leaves. You can imagine how amazed she was when she saw a little elf sitting in the very center of the flower, as white and transparent as if he were made of glass. He had a tiny gold crown on his head and bright wings on his shoulders, and he was scarcely any bigger than Thumbelina. He was the elf of the flower. In every flower there lived some little man or woman, but this was the king of them all.

"How handsome he is!" whispered Thumbelina to the swallow.

The little king was quite frightened by the swallow, for to him it was a gigantic bird, but when he saw Thumbelina he was delighted. She was certainly the prettiest girl he had ever seen. He took his gold crown from his head and put it on hers, asking her name and begging her to be his wife, for then she could be the queen of the flowers.

Now, this was more like it—a real husband, very different from the son of a toad, or a mole in his black fur coat. So she said yes to the handsome king, and out from every flower came a lord or a lady elf, all so graceful that it was a joy to behold them.

At the wedding everyone brought Thumbelina a present, but the best present of all was a pair of pretty wings from a large white fly. They were fastened to Thumbelina's back, so she could fly from flower to flower. There was great merrymaking, and the swallow sat

overhead in his nest and sang to them as well as he could, but at heart he was distressed, for he loved Thumbelina and would have liked to be with her always.

"Farewell, farewell!" sang the swallow a little later, and he flew away again from the warm land—far, far away back to Denmark. There the swallow has a little nest above the window of a man who tells fairy tales. The swallow sang and told the storyteller this very story.

The Little
Swineherd

HERE was once a poor Prince. He had a kingdom, but it was a very little one. Nevertheless, it was large enough to impress a princess, and he was determined to marry the Emperor's daughter. The Prince's name was known far and wide, and there were hundreds of princesses who would have been very glad to marry him, if they had been asked. But did the Emperor's daughter accept his advances? Well, now, you shall soon find out.

On the grave of the Prince's father grew a rose tree—a very lovely rose tree. It bloomed only once every five years, and then it bore only a single rose, but that one rose was so sweet that by merely smelling it people forgot their cares and sorrows. The Prince also had a nightingale that could sing as though all the lovely songs in the world were in its little throat. He wished the Princess to have both the rose and the nightingale, so they were both put into silver cases and sent to her.

The Emperor had the silver cases carried before him into the large room where the Princess liked to play with her ladies-in-waiting. When she saw the cases with the presents in them, the Princess clapped her hands for joy.

"Just imagine if it is a little pussycat!" said she. But it turned out to be a rose tree with a single beautiful rose.

"How prettily it is made!" said all the Court ladies.

"It is more than pretty," said the Emperor. "It is elegant."

But the Princess felt the rose and immediately was ready to burst into tears. "Fie, Papa," she said. "It is not artificial after all—it is *real!*"

"Fie!" said all the Court ladies. "It is real!"

"Let us see what is in the other case before we lose our tempers," said the Emperor, and so the nightingale was produced, and it sang so sweetly that for the moment it was quite impossible to find any fault with it.

"Superbe! Charmant!" cried the Court ladies, for they all chattered in French. It was hard to say which of them chattered worst.

"The bird reminds me of the late Empress's music box," said an old courtier. "Ah, yes. It's the same tune, and the same rhythm."

"Yes," said the Emperor, and he began to cry like a child.

"But it is not a real bird, I hope," said the Princess.

"Yes, it is a real bird," said the courtiers who had brought it.

"Indeed! Then let it fly away," said the Princess, and she would not, under any circumstances, permit the Prince to come see her.

But the Prince was determined to meet the Princess. He dressed in ragged clothes and smeared his face with black mud, pulled his cap down over his eyes, and knocked at the palace door.

"Good morning, Emperor," he said. "Could I work here in the palace?"

"Well, there are so many applicants already," said the Emperor, "but let me see. I very much want someone who can look after the swine, for we have lots of them."

So the Prince was appointed the Imperial swineherd. They gave him a wretched little shed close to the pigsty, where he had to live. Now the Prince was very talented at making things. All day long,

when he was not busy with the pigs, he sat and worked, and by evening had made a pretty little clay pot, with bells fastened all around it. When the pot began to boil, the bells tinkled prettily, and played the old melody—

"Ah! thou darling, Augustine!
'Tis all over now, I ween!"

But best of all was that when anyone held his or her fingers near the steam that rose from the pot, immediately he or she could smell what was being cooked in every kitchen in the town. Now, that was certainly more impressive than a rose.

Just as the Prince had finished making the pot, the Princess came walking along with her ladies-in-waiting. When she heard the melody she stood still, and was delighted, for she was able to play "Ah! thou darling Augustine!" on the piano. Indeed, it was the only tune she knew, and she played it with one finger.

"Yes," she said, "that is the song that I can play. He must indeed be a clever swineherd. Go in and ask him what the instrument costs."

So one of the ladies went down into the shed, but she put on boots first. "Tell me, what instrument is playing that song?" she asked the swineherd.

"The bells on my little clay pot play the melody when the pot boils."

"What do you want for that pot?" asked the lady.

"I want ten kisses from the Princess," said the swineherd.

"Good gracious!" said the lady.

"Yes, and I will not take less," said the swineherd.

"Well, what did he say?" asked the Princess, when she returned.

"I really dare not tell you," said the lady-in-waiting. "It is too frightful!"

"Then whisper it in my ear." So she whispered.

"He is very naughty, really," said the Princess, and turned away at

29

once. But when she had gone a little distance the bells jingled again so sweetly—

"Ah! thou darling Augustine!
'Tis all over now, I ween!"

"Listen now," said the Princess. "Ask him if he will take ten kisses from my Court ladies."

"No, thank you," said the swineherd. "I must have ten kisses from the Princess, please, or I shall keep the pot."

"How very boring, to be sure," said the Princess. "Well, then all of you stand in front of me, so that nobody can see!"

So all the Court ladies made a circle around them, spreading out their dresses, and the swineherd got the ten kisses, and the Princess got the pot.

The Court ladies and the Princess had a merry time. All that evening, and the whole next day, the pot was kept boiling. There was not a kitchen in the town that they didn't know what was being cooked there, whether it was the Lord Chamberlain's or the cobbler's. The Court ladies danced and clapped their hands.

"We know who is going to have soup and pancakes for dinner, and who is going to have chops and hasty pudding. How interesting that is!"

"Why, it is most highly interesting," said the Lady Stewardess of the Household.

"Yes, but hold your tongues about it, for I am the Emperor's daughter."

"Of course, of course," they all said.

The swineherd, that is to say, the Prince—but *they* of course thought he was a real swineherd—let no day pass without making something or other. One day he made a rattle, which, when spun, played all the waltzes, jigs, and polkas that ever were known since the creation of the world.

"Why, that is *superbe!*" said the Princess as she passed by. "I have

never heard a finer composition. Listen now. Just go and ask him what the instrument costs. But mind, I will give no more kisses."

"He wants a hundred kisses from the Princess," said the lady who had gone to ask.

"I think he is mad," said the Princess, and she went on her way. But when she had gone a little distance she stood still. "After all, one should encourage the fine arts," she said. "I am the Emperor's daughter. Tell him he shall have ten kisses as before. He can take the rest from my Court ladies."

"But we do not want to kiss him," said the Court ladies.

"Fiddlesticks," said the Princess. "If I can kiss him, surely you may. Remember, I give you board and wages." So the lady had to go to him again.

"A hundred kisses from the Princess," he said. "That is all I will accept."

"Stand around us then," said the Princess. All the Court ladies did as they were bid, and the swineherd began his hundred kisses.

"What is the meaning of all that commotion by the pigsty?" asked the Emperor, who had stepped out on the balcony. He rubbed his eyes and put on his spectacles. "Why, if it isn't the Court ladies. They are playing some sort of game. I must go down to them." So he put on his slippers.

My goodness, what a hurry he was in.

As soon as he came into the courtyard, he walked very softly, and the Court ladies were so busy counting the kisses—so that it would be a perfectly fair bargain and the swineherd would not get too many or too few—that they never noticed the Emperor.

He stood on tiptoe. "Why, what's this?" he asked, when he saw the Princess and the swineherd kissing, and he began to swat them about the heads with his slipper just as the swineherd had got his eighty-sixth kiss.

"Be off with you, out of my sight!" said the Emperor, for he was very angry, and both the Princess and the swineherd were expelled from his kingdom.

The Princess stood weeping, the swineherd cursed, and the rain poured down in torrents.

"Alas, wretched creature that I am!" said the Princess. "If only I had agreed to meet that nice Prince. Alas, how miserable I am."

The swineherd slipped behind a tree, wiped all the mud from his face, threw away his dirty clothes, and stepped forward in his princely garments, looking so handsome that the Princess could not help but curtsy.

"I no longer want to marry you," he said. "You would not have an honest Prince. You could not appreciate a marvelous rose or a wonderful nightingale. But you would kiss a swineherd to get a foolish toy. Take it, then, and much good may it do you."

The Prince returned to his kingdom, shut the palace door behind him, and bolted it. The Princess was left in the rain singing:

"Ah! thou Darling Augustine!
'Tis all over now, I ween!"

The Emperor's
New Clothes

ANY years ago there lived an Emperor who was so fond of new clothes that he spent all his money on dress and finery. He cared not a whit for his soldiers, nor for going to the theater, nor for driving in the park. All he really cared about was showing off his new clothes. He had a coat for every hour of the day, and just as in other countries they speak of the "King in Council Meeting," here they spoke of the "Emperor in His Dressing Room."

The great city where he lived was a pleasant place and many strangers visited it. One day two men arrived who claimed to be weavers. They said they knew how to weave the most beautiful cloth imaginable. Not only were the colors and patterns altogether extraordinary, they said, but the clothes made from such cloth had the peculiar property of being invisible to every person who was either unfit for his office or stupid.

These would indeed be valuable clothes, thought the Emperor. By wearing them, I could find out which of my ministers are unfit for the posts they occupy, and I could tell the wise from the stupid. Yes, some of that cloth must be woven for me at once. And he gave the two men a lot of money in advance so that they could begin their work.

They immediately set up two looms and pretended they were working, but there was absolutely nothing on the looms. Very soon they demanded the finest silk and the purest gold thread, which they put carefully away, then continued working on the empty looms until late into the night.

I would like to know how the manufacture of the cloth is coming along, thought the Emperor, but really and truly his heart felt uneasy when he remembered that the stupid or the incapable would not be able to see the cloth. He fancied, indeed, that he had no need to be anxious on his own account, but he thought it would be safer to send someone else first to see how things were going. Every person in the city had heard of the wonderful properties of the new cloth, and they were all eager to see how foolish or stupid their neighbors were.

I will send my worthy old minister to the weavers, thought the Emperor. He can best see what the cloth looks like, for he is a man of intellect, and none is fitter for his office than he.

So the able old minister went into the room where the two impostors sat working at the empty looms.

Mercy on us! he thought, and opened his eyes very wide. I can't see anything. But he took good care not to say so.

The two impostors begged him to come closer, and asked him if the pattern was not a pretty one, and the colors beautiful. Then they pointed at the empty looms and the poor old minister opened his eyes wider and wider, but he could see nothing, for there was nothing to see.

Good gracious! he thought. I am surely not stupid. I never thought so before, and I'll take good care that nobody will know it now. What! I am not fit for my office, eh? Oh, no, it will never do for me to go and say that I can't see the cloth.

"Well, have you nothing to say about it?" said one of the weavers to the old minister.

"Oh, it is beautiful, absolutely the loveliest thing in the world," said the old minister, and he took out his spectacles. "What a pattern!

And those colors, too! Yes, I'll tell the Emperor that it pleases me immensely."

"Well, we are pleased with it, too," said the two weavers, and then they named the colors in detail, and described the pattern. The old minister carefully listened to all they said, so he would be able to repeat the same things to the Emperor, which he did.

And now the impostors demanded more money, more silk, and more gold. They needed the gold for the weaving, they said, though they really stuck everything into their own pockets. Not so much as a thread passed over the looms, but they continued as before to weave upon the empty looms.

In a short time the Emperor sent another very able official to see how the weaving was progressing, and if the cloth was nearly ready. Like the minister, he gazed and gazed, but as there was nothing there but the empty loom, he could not see anything.

"A pretty piece of cloth, isn't it?" said the two impostors, and they pretended to point out the pretty patterns, although there was really no trace of them.

Surely I am not stupid, thought the man. Not fit for my post, eh!

A pretty joke, I must say, but I must not let it be noticed. So he praised the cloth he did not see and congratulated them on the beautiful colors and the lovely patterns. "Yes, the cloth is perfectly enchanting," he said to the Emperor.

Soon all the people in the town were talking about the splendid cloth.

Finally the Emperor decided he must see the cloth himself while it was still on the loom. With several of the great folk of his realm, including the two able officials who had been there before, he went to the two crafty impostors, who were now working with all their might, but without either a stitch or thread.

"Now, is it not magnificent?" exclaimed the two officials. "Will Your Majesty observe what patterns, what colors are here?" They pointed at the empty looms, taking it for granted that the others could see the cloth.

Why, what is this? thought the Emperor. I don't see anything! How horrible! Am I stupid then? Am I unfit to be Emperor? That would be the most frightful thing that could happen to me.

"Oh, it is very fine," he said aloud. "It has my most gracious approval," and he nodded his head and gazed at the empty loom. He would not say that he could not see anything.

His whole entourage stared and stared. They could see no more of it than the others, but they repeated after the Emperor, "Oh, it is very fine," and advised him to wear clothes made of this new and gorgeous cloth for the first time on the occasion of the grand procession that was about to take place.

"It is magnificent, elegant, excellent." The words were repeated by each member of the entourage. Everybody seemed so mightily pleased with the cloth that the Emperor gave each of the impostors a ribbon and a medal to wear, and conferred on them the title of "Weavers to the Imperial Court."

On the eve of the procession the impostors sat up all night and had more than sixty candles lit. The people could see that they were busy

making the Emperor's new clothes. They pretended to take the cloth from the loom, they clipped the air with large scissors, and sewed with needles without thread. At last one of them declared, "There, the clothes are now ready!"

The Emperor, with his principal lords, then came himself, and the impostors raised their arms as if they were holding something up, and said, "Look, here are the stockings, and here is the coat, and here is the cap. They are as light as gossamer," they continued. "You would imagine you had nothing on at all, but that is just the beauty of the cloth."

"Of course!" said all the gentlemen-in-waiting, but they could see nothing, for there was nothing to see.

"And now, if Your Imperial Majesty would most graciously deign to have your clothes taken off," said the impostors, "we will put on the new ones for Your Majesty. In front of the large mirror, please. Thank you!"

So the Emperor's clothes were removed, and the impostors pretended to give him the newly made ones piece by piece, and they smoothed down his body and attached something that was supposed to be the train, and the Emperor turned and twisted himself in front of the mirror.

"What a wonderful suit it is! How nicely it fits," the people cried with one voice. "What a pattern! What colors! It is a splendid outfit!"

"The canopy that is to be carried over Your Majesty in the procession is waiting outside," the master of ceremonies announced.

"All right," said the Emperor. "I am quite ready. Do my clothes fit well?" He turned himself once more before the mirror, to make believe that he was now taking a general survey of his splendor. The gentlemen-in-waiting, who had to carry his train, fumbled with their hands along the floor as if they were picking up the train, and as they went along they held their hands in the air, for they dared not let it be supposed that they saw nothing.

And so the Emperor marched in the procession beneath the beau-

tiful canopy, and everyone in the streets and in the windows said, "Gracious, how perfect the Emperor's new clothes are. What a beautiful train. How splendidly everything fits." No one would have it thought that he saw nothing, for then he would certainly have been declared unfit for his post, or very stupid. None of the Emperor's clothes had been so successful as these.

"Why, he has got nothing on!" cried a little child.

"Listen to the voice of innocence," said the father, for everyone was whispering to his neighbor what the child had said. "He has nothing on! There is a little child here who says he has nothing on!"

"He really has nothing on," cried the whole crowd at last.

The Emperor shrank within himself as he heard the crowd. It certainly seemed to him that they were right, but at the same time he thought, At any rate I must go through with this procession to the end. So he put on an even haughtier air, and the gentlemen-in-waiting marched behind, carefully holding up the train that wasn't there.

The Nightingale

ONG ago in China there lived a great Emperor. His palace was the most gorgeous in the world. It was built entirely of the finest porcelain and was very costly, but so fragile that everyone always had to take particular care not to touch it. In the garden were the most wonderful flowers. Silver bells were tied to the most beautiful of them and they rang whenever anybody passed by, so no one would miss seeing the flowers. Yes, everything in the Emperor's garden was extremely beautiful, and the garden itself stretched so far that the gardener himself did not know where it ended.

Far into the garden were the loveliest woods, with tall trees and deep lakes. The forest reached all the way to the sea, which was deep and blue. Large ships could sail under the branches of the trees. In one of these branches lived a nightingale that sang so sweetly that even the poor fisherman, who had many other things to attend to, would stop to listen. "How beautifully the nightingale sings," he said, but then he would get busy with other things and forget the bird. Yet, the next night, when it sang again and the fisherman came near, he would say the same thing: "How beautifully the nightingale sings!"

Travelers came from all over the world to see and admire the

Emperor's city and the palace and the garden. But when they heard the nightingale they said, "Yes, this is better than anything in the city."

When they got home the travelers described what they had seen and wrote many books about the city and the palace and the garden. But they did not forget the nightingale: indeed, they put that first, and those who could write poetry penned the loveliest verses about the nightingale in the woods by the deep blue lake.

These books were read around the world and some of them eventually reached the Emperor. He sat on his gold throne and read and read. Every moment he nodded his head, for it pleased him to read the fine descriptions of his city and palace and garden. "But when all is said, the nightingale is still the best of all!" said the books.

"Why, what is this?" said the Emperor—"the nightingale? I do not know of any nightingale. I had no idea there was such a bird in my kingdom, let alone in my very garden. Must one learn such things from books? This must be looked into."

So he called his lord-in-waiting, who was so grand that whenever anyone lower in rank spoke to him or asked a question he only answered, "P!" which meant nothing at all.

"There is said to be a very remarkable bird called a nightingale!" the Emperor informed him. "People declare that it is the finest thing in my vast realm. Why have I not been told about it?"

"I have never heard it so much as mentioned before," replied the lord-in-waiting. "It has never been presented at Court!"

"I command it to come here this very evening and sing to me," said the Emperor. "Why, the whole world knows what I possess and yet *I* don't know it!"

"I never heard the name of it before!" said the lord-in-waiting, "but I will have inquiries made and find it!"

But where was it to be found? The lord-in-waiting ran up and down all the staircases in the palace and through all the rooms and corridors, but no one he met knew anything about the nightingale.

 45

So the lord-in-waiting came back to the Emperor and said the whole thing must be a fable invented by those who wrote books. "Your Imperial Majesty must not believe what you find written there. It is all made up!"

"But the book in which I read this was sent to me by the high and mighty Emperor of Japan," said the Emperor, "and therefore it cannot be an untruth. I wish to hear the nightingale. It must be here this evening! And if it does not come, the whole Court shall be executed immediately after supper."

"*Tsing pe!*" said the lord-in-waiting, and again he ran up and down all the stairs, through all the rooms and corridors, and half the Court ran with him, for they did not like the idea of being executed. They asked everyone they passed about the wonderful nightingale that was known to all the rest of the world but not to anybody at Court.

At last they found a poor little girl in the kitchen and she said, "What, the nightingale? Why, I know it quite well. Sing? I should think so! Every evening I take the leftovers from dinner to my poor sick mother who lives near the seashore, and when I am on my way back and am tired and stop to rest in the woods I hear the nightingale sing, and then the tears come into my eyes and it is just as if my mother were kissing me!"

"Little scullery maid!" said the lord-in-waiting, "I will get you a permanent position in the kitchen, with permission to watch the Emperor eat, if you will lead us to the nightingale, for it must sing for the Emperor this very evening."

So they went together to the woods where the scullery maid heard the nightingale sing. Half the Court went along. As they picked their way through the woods, a cow began to moo.

"Oh!" said the lord-in-waiting. "Now we have it! That is really a remarkable power for so small an animal! Of course, we have heard it before. We remember it distinctly!"

"No, that is the mooing of a cow," said the little scullery maid. "We are still a long way from the place!"

Then the frogs croaked in the marshes.

"Pretty!" said the Chinese court chaplain. "Now I hear it. It is just like tiny temple bells."

"No, those are the frogs," said the little scullery maid. "But I think we shall hear it very soon."

Then the nightingale began to sing.

"That's it!" said the little girl. "Listen, listen! And look, there it sits," and she pointed to a little gray bird in the branches.

"Is it possible?" asked the lord-in-waiting. "I never imagined it was like that. How very simple it looks."

"Little nightingale," cried the scullery maid loudly, "our gracious Emperor wants you to sing to him so much."

"With the greatest pleasure," said the nightingale, and it sang so that it was a delight to listen.

"It is like crystal bells," said the lord-in-waiting, "and just look how the little throat moves up and down. It is really remarkable. We have never heard it before. It will have a great success at Court!"

"Shall I sing to the Emperor once more?" asked the nightingale, for it thought the Emperor was one of those listening.

"My excellent little nightingale," said the lord-in-waiting, "it is my privilege to invite you to a great entertainment at Court this evening, where you will enchant His High Imperial Majesty with your charming voice!"

"It sounds best in the green woods," said the nightingale, but it willingly went with them when it heard that the Emperor wished it.

There were grand doings at the palace. The porcelain walls and floor shone with the lights of thousands of gold lamps, the loveliest flowers were set up in the corridors, and there was a great commotion with all the bells ringing.

In the middle of the large room where the Emperor sat, a golden perch had been placed for the nightingale to sit upon. The whole Court was there and the little scullery maid was allowed to stand behind the door and listen. All the ladies and gentlemen wore their

most gorgeous finery and all turned their eyes to the little gray bird when the Emperor nodded to it.

Then the nightingale sang so beautifully that tears came into the Emperor's eyes and trickled right down his cheeks. Then it sang more beautifully than ever, so that the notes seemed to go to the very heart of the listener. The Emperor was so delighted that he offered to give the nightingale his gold slipper to wear around its neck. But the nightingale declined with thanks. It had been well rewarded already, it said.

"I have seen tears in the eyes of the Emperor, and that is the most precious treasure to me. An Emperor's tears have a wonderful power. Goodness knows I have been rewarded enough," and the nightingale sang again, its voice sweet and heavenly.

"That is the most captivating music we have ever heard," said all the ladies. Even the footmen and maids-in-waiting said that they were impressed, and that is a great deal, for they are always the most difficult to please. Yes, the nightingale's success was complete.

The nightingale agreed to remain at Court, to have its own cage and the privilege of going outside twice in the daytime and once at night. It was attended by twelve servants, each of whom tied a silk ribbon around its leg and held on tightly. There was not very much enjoyment in such a walk as that!

The whole town talked about the remarkable bird and whenever two people met, one of them immediately said to the other, "Night!" and the other said "gale!" and then they sighed and understood each other. Indeed, eleven children were named after it, but not one of them could sing a single musical note.

One day a large package arrived for the Emperor. On the outside of it was written, THE NIGHTINGALE.

"Here now we have a new book about our famous bird," said the Emperor. But when the package was opened the Emperor discovered it was not really a book but a little work of art, which lay in a box, an artificial nightingale that had been made to resemble the

living one but was covered with diamonds, rubies, and sapphires. As soon as this artificial bird was wound up, it could sing one of the pieces the real nightingale sang, and its neck moved up and down and all the gold and silver on it sparkled. Around its neck was a little ribbon and a small card. On this was written: "The Emperor of Japan's nightingale is poor indeed when compared with that of the Emperor of China."

"That is very pretty," everyone said, and the messenger who had brought the artificial bird immediately received the title of Chief Imperial Nightingale-Bringer.

"Now the two nightingales must sing together," said the courtiers. "What a duet it will be!"

But the two birds could not sing together at all, for the real nightingale sang in his own way and the artificial bird went by clockwork. "I have no fault to find with it," said the music master. "Its singing is perfect in my opinion." So the artificial bird was set to sing alone. It sang just as beautifully as the real one and was much prettier to look at besides—it glistened like bracelets and rings.

Then it sang the same piece thirty-three times and still wasn't tired. The people would have liked to hear it all over again, but the Emperor thought that the living bird should have a turn now to sing a little—but where was it? Nobody had noticed that it had flown out of the open window back to its green woods.

"Did you ever hear of such a thing!" said the Emperor, and all the courtiers got very angry and declared that the nightingale was a most ungrateful creature.

"At any rate we still have the best bird," they said, and so the artificial bird had to sing again, and that made the thirty-fourth time they had heard the same piece. But even then they did not know all of it, for it was so very difficult. The music master praised the bird beyond measure, announcing that it was better than the real nightingale, not only with regard to its clothes and the many beautiful diamonds, but also as to its own merit.

 50

"For look now, Your Imperial Majesty, and you also, ladies and gentlemen, with the real nightingale you can never tell for certain what note will come, but with the artificial bird everything is fixed and definite. You can explain all about it. You can open it and display the ingenuity of man. You can see the position of the various parts, how they work and how they follow one after the other."

 51

"Those are exactly my own thoughts," said all present, and the music master got permission to show the bird to the rest of the people of the kingdom on the following Sunday.

"They also shall hear it sing," said the Emperor.

And hear it they did and were as pleased as if they had been to a tea party and drunk lots of tea. They all said, "Oh!" and nodded in approval, but the poor fisherman who had heard the real nightingale said, "It sounds nice enough, but there is something missing. I do not know what."

The real nightingale was banished from the realm.

The artificial bird was placed on a silk cushion right next to the Emperor's bed. All the gifts it had received, both of gold and precious stones, lay around it, and as for titles, why, it was now known as "High Imperial Night Singer." And the music master wrote twenty-five books about the artificial bird. His treatise was long and learned and full of the hardest words, and all the people said they had read and understood it, for otherwise they would have been considered stupid.

A whole year passed. The Emperor, the Court, and all the other Chinese knew by heart every little cluck in the artificial bird's song, but just for that reason they liked it all the better. They could sing it, too, and they did so. The street boys sang, "Zee-zee-zee! Kluk-kluk-kluk!" and the Emperor sang it. Yes, indeed, it was really charming!

But one evening, while the artificial bird was singing its best and the Emperor was lying in bed listening to it, something inside the bird said "sooop" and something went "muurrrr!" All the wheels ran around and the music stopped.

The Emperor sprang out of bed and sent for his physician, but what could *he* do! Then he called the watchmaker, who after a good deal of talking and tinkering repaired the bird somewhat. But he said they must play it sparingly because the machinery was so worn that it was not possible to supply new parts that could be relied upon to make the music. It was a great tragedy. Only once a year could the

artificial bird be allowed to sing and they were very strict about it even then. The music master made a little speech full of big words and said that it was just as good as before, and so it *was* just as good as before.

Five years passed by, and the whole land was bowed down by a great sorrow, for they were all devoted to their Emperor, and now he was sick and could not live, it was said. A new Emperor had already been chosen and the people stood in the street and asked the lord-in-waiting how their Emperor was doing.

"P!" said he and shook his head.

Cold and pale, the Emperor lay in his large bed. The whole Court thought he was dead and everyone ran to greet the new Emperor. The servants left his bedside, and cloth coverings were strewn about the floors so that people would walk softly in respect. Therefore all was quiet and still, oh, so still. But the Emperor was not dead yet. Stiff and pale he lay in his gorgeous bed with the long velvet curtains and the heavy gold tassels. High above, a window stood open and the moon shone in upon the Emperor and the artificial bird.

The poor Emperor could scarcely breathe. It was as if someone were sitting on his chest. He opened his eyes and saw that it was Death who sat upon his heart and had taken his gold crown. In one hand Death held the Emperor's golden sword and in the other his splendid banner. And all around the folds of the large velvet bed curtains strange-looking heads peeped out, some quite ugly and others sweet and gentle—they were the Emperor's good and evil deeds gazing at him now that Death was at his heart.

"Music, music!" cried the Emperor. "Sound the big Chinese drum, so that I do not hear what they say!"

But the figures remained and Death nodded.

"Music, music!" shrieked the Emperor. "You charming little gold bird, sing, sing, please do. I have given you gold and precious things. I have hung my gold slipper around your neck. Sing, I say, sing!"

But the bird remained silent, for there was no one to wind it up and it never sang otherwise. And Death kept on looking at the Emperor, and all was so still, so frightfully still.

At that very instant the most beautiful song sounded near the window. It came from the little living nightingale, which sat upon the branch outside. It had heard of the Emperor's dire need and had come to sing hope and comfort to his soul, and as it sang the shapes around the bed grew paler and paler, the blood moved more quickly through the Emperor's weak limbs, and Death himself listened and said, "Go on, little nightingale, go on!"

"Yes, but will you give me the splendid gold sword? Will you give me the rich banner? Will you give me the Emperor's crown?" said the nightingale.

And Death gave away all these treasures for a song, and the nightingale kept on singing. It sang of the silent churchyard where the white roses grow, where the elderberry tree scents the air, and where the fresh grass is wet with mourners' tears. Then Death felt a longing for his garden and swept out the window like a cold white mist.

"Thank you, thank you!" said the Emperor. "You heavenly little bird. I know you well. I drove you out of my kingdom and yet you have sung the evil visions away from my bedside. How can I reward you?"

"You *have* rewarded me," said the nightingale. "I drew tears from your eyes the first time I sang. That I shall never forget—those are jewels that bring joy to a singer's heart. But go to sleep now and get well and strong. I will sing to you."

As the nightingale sang the Emperor fell into a sweet sleep, a soft, refreshing sleep.

The sun was shining in upon him through all the windows when he awoke, strong and full of health. Not one of his servants had yet come back, for they thought he was dead, but the nightingale still sang and sang.

"You must stay with me always," said the Emperor. "You shall only sing when you like and I will break the artificial bird into a thousand pieces."

"Don't do that!" said the nightingale. "After all, it did what it could. Keep it as before. For myself, I cannot make my nest in the palace, but let me come when I wish and then I will sit on this branch near the window in the evening and sing to you. I will make you thoughtful and happy at the same time. I will sing of those who rejoice and of those who suffer. I will sing of the good and the evil that go on around you and yet are hidden from you. The little songbird flies far and wide. He flies to the poor fisherman, to the roof of the farmer, to everyone who is far from you and your Court. I'll come, I'll sing to you—but one thing you *must* promise me!"

"I'll promise you everything," said the Emperor, and there he stood in his Imperial robes, which he had put on himself, and he held his sword, heavy with gold, to his heart.

"One thing I beg of you! Tell no one that you have a little bird that tells you everything."

And away the nightingale flew.

The servants came in to see their dead Emperor. Yes, there they all stood, and how amazed they were when the Emperor sat up and said, "Good morning!"

 56

The Ugly Duckling

T WAS so pretty out in the country in the glorious summertime. The corn was yellow, the oats green; the hay was stacked in the meadows, and the stork strode about on his long red legs and chattered Egyptian, for he had learned that language from his mother. All around the fields and meadows were great forests, and in the midst of the woods were deep lakes. Yes, it was delightful in the country.

In the sunlight stood an old country house surrounded by deep ditches. From the walls right down to the water grew large plants that had shot up so high that little children could stand on tiptoe beneath the tallest leaves. In this lonesome spot, a duck sat upon her nest, waiting for her young to hatch. By this time she was growing tired of the task. It was taking so long and she seldom received visitors. The other ducks preferred to swim about in the ditches and rarely waddled up the bank to sit under a leaf and gossip with her.

At last one egg cracked, and then another and another.

"Peep! Peep!" was the cry as the baby ducklings stuck out their little heads.

"Quick! Quick!" cried the mother duck. So they all scampered around as fast as they could to explore their world beneath the green leaves.

"How big the world is, to be sure!" said one of the young ducklings, for now, indeed, they had much more room to stir about than when they lay in their eggshells.

"Do you think that this is the whole world?" asked their mother. "Why, it stretches far beyond the other side of the garden right into the parson's field, but I have never been there. I suppose the whole lot of you have finally hatched, eh?" and she rose up. "No, I haven't got you all yet. The biggest egg is still there. How much longer must I wait? I am sick and tired of it!" And down she sat again.

"Well, how are things with you?" asked an old duck who came to pay her a visit.

"This last egg is taking such a long time!" answered the sitting duck. "No one is cracking through. But just look at the others! They are the prettiest ducklings I have ever seen. They are still just like their father."

"Let me see the egg that won't crack," said the old duck. "Take my word for it, it's a turkey's egg. I was fooled that way myself once, and the youngsters were a worry and a trouble to me, I can tell you, for they were afraid of the water. I couldn't get them into it no matter how hard I tried. I snapped and quacked, but it was of no use. Let me see the egg, I say. Yes, it *is* a turkey's egg. Leave it alone and go and teach the other children to swim!"

"No, I'll sit on it a bit longer," said the duck. "I have sat so long already, I may as well sit a few hours longer."

"As you like," said the old duck, and she waddled off.

At last the big egg cracked. "Peep, peep!" said the fledgling as it wriggled out—he was so big and ugly. The duck looked at him.

"What a frightfully big duckling he is!" she cried. "None of the others is a bit like him. Surely, he cannot be a turkey chick. Well, we shall soon find out about that. Into the water he goes if I have to *push* him in."

The next day the weather was glorious. The sun shone on all the green leaves as the mother duck and her family came down to the

ditch. "Quick! Quick!" she cried, as one duckling after another plunged into the water. The water covered their heads, but up they bobbed again and floated so prettily—their legs knew just what to do. All of them were in the water. Even the ugly gray fledgling swam along with them.

"No, he is no turkey," said the mother duck. "See how nicely he uses his legs, how upright he holds himself! He is my own child. Now, really, when you look closely, he's quite pretty. Quick! Quick! Come with me now and I will lead you into the great world and present you to the duckyard. But always keep close to me so that no one will step on you—and beware of the cat!"

So they came into the duckyard. There was a frightful noise there, for two duck families were fighting over an eel's head, and in the end the cat got it.

"Look, that is the way of the world," said the mother duck, licking her beak, for she would have liked the eel's head herself. "Use your legs," she said. "Look smart and nod your necks at that old duck over there, for she is the most distinguished one here. She is of Spanish descent, and do you see that red tag tied to her leg? That is the greatest distinction any duck can have—it is as much as to say they don't want to get rid of her, and men and beasts are to take note. Quack! Quack! Don't turn your feet in! A well-brought-up duckling keeps his feet wide apart like his father and mother. Look! And now thrust out your neck and say 'Quack!' "

They did so, but all the other ducks looked at them and said quite loudly, "Just look! Now we shall have all that mob too. As if there were not enough of us here already. And oh, fie! What a fright *that* duckling looks. We certainly won't put up with him." And immediately a duck flew at the big fledgling and bit him in the neck.

"Leave him alone," said the mother duck. "He's doing no harm."

"Yes, but he is so big and strange," said the duck who had bitten him.

"You have pretty children, mother," said the old duck with the

red rag around her leg. "They are all pretty except that one, which hasn't turned out well at all. I wish you could make him over again."

"Impossible," said the mother of the ducklings. "He is not pretty, but he has a good disposition and swims as nicely as any of the others—I may say even a bit better. I'm sure he will grow prettier, or perhaps somewhat smaller, in time. He has been in the egg too long and therefore he has not got the proper shape."

Then she trimmed the ruffled feathers of his neck with her beak and smoothed down the rest of him. "Besides, he is a drake," she said, "and so it doesn't matter so much. I think he'll be strong enough to fight his way along."

"Your other ducklings are very nice," said the old duck. "Make yourself at home, and if you find an eel's head you may bring it to me."

And so the family made themselves comfortable. But the poor duckling who had come out of the egg last of all, and looked so ugly, was bitten, pushed about, and made fun of by both the ducks and the hens. "He is too big," they all cried, and the turkey cock, who had been born with spurs and therefore thought himself an emperor at least, puffed himself out like a ship in full sail, slammed into the poor duckling, and then gabbled until he was red in the face. The duckling did not know where to turn and was so distressed because he was ugly and the laughingstock of the whole duckyard.

This was only the first day. After that things grew worse and worse. The ugly duckling was tormented by them all. His own brothers and sisters kept saying, "If only the cat would take you, you hideous object," while even his own mother said, "If only you were far, far away!" The ducks bit him, the hens pecked him, and the girl who gave the birds their food kicked him.

Finally he decided to run away, so he flew right over the hedge. The little birds in the bushes were frightened and flew into the air. "That is because I am so ugly," said the duckling and closed his eyes. He ran on until he came to a large marsh, where the wild ducks lived.

There he lay the whole night, weary and sorrowful.

In the morning the wild ducks flew up into the air and saw their new comrade. "What kind of a thing are you?" they asked, and the duckling turned in every direction and greeted them as well as he could.

"You are intensely ugly," said the wild ducks. "But it is all the same to us as long as you do not marry into the family!"

Poor creature! As if he had any idea of marrying. All he wanted was to be allowed to lie among the rushes and drink a little swamp water.

There he lay for two whole days. Then along came two wild geese, or rather wild ganders, who were recently hatched and full of mischief.

"Listen, comrade!" they said. "You are so ugly that we have quite taken a fancy to you. Will you play with us? Near here, in another marsh, are some sweet, delightful wild geese who can say 'Quack!' most charmingly. You'll be able to make friends there, ugly as you are!"

"Pop! Pop!" they heard at the same instant, and the two wild geese fell dead among the rushes. "Pop! Pop!" sounded again, and flocks of wild geese flew up from the rushes. Then there were more bangs. It was a shooting party. The sportsmen were hiding in the marsh grasses. Some even sat in the branches of the trees that stretched right over the rushes. The blue gunsmoke hovered like clouds among the dark trees and hung far over the water, and the hunting dogs came splash-splashing through the mud. Reeds and rushes swayed in every direction. It was a terrible moment for the poor duckling, who turned his head around to hide it beneath his wing. At the same instant a frightful big dog appeared, his tongue hanging far out of his mouth, his eyes shining fearfully. He put his jaws right against the duckling, showed his sharp teeth—and splash! Off went the dog without seizing the duckling.

"Oh, heaven be praised," sighed the duckling. "I am so ugly that

even the dog doesn't want to bite me." And he lay quite still while the shots hissed among the tall grasses and gun after gun cracked and banged.

Only when many hours had passed and all was quiet again did the poor duckling dare to get up. He waited even longer before he looked around and then hurried away from the swamp as fast as he could. He ran over marsh and meadow, but there was such a strong wind that he could hardly make any headway.

Toward evening the duckling reached a broken-down little cottage. The poor cottage was so ramshackle that it could not decide on which side it should fall first, and so remained standing. The door was off one of its hinges and hung so loosely that the duckling could peek into the room through the crack.

An old woman lived here with her cat and her hen. The cat, whom she called Sonny, could arch his back and purr. He could even throw out sparks, but you had to stroke his fur the wrong way first. The hen had stumpy little legs and was called Chicky-short-legs. She laid good eggs and the old woman loved her as if she had been her child.

The next morning they all noticed the strange duckling, and the cat began to purr and the hen to cluck.

"Well, I never," said the old woman, and looked all about her. But her eyesight was not very good, so she thought the duckling was a fat duck that had lost its way. "Why, this is a rare good find," she said. "Now perhaps I can have ducks' eggs, too. We must wait a bit and see."

So the duckling stayed with them for three weeks, but not a single egg appeared. The cat was master in that house and the hen was mistress, and they always said, "We and the world!" for they thought that they were half of the world, and the better half, too. The duckling hinted that there might be two opinions on this point, but the hen would not hear of such a thing.

"Can you lay eggs?" she asked.

"No."

"Then hold your tongue!"

And the cat said, "Can you arch your back, purr, and throw out sparks?"

"No."

"Then you have no business having any opinion at all when sensible people are talking."

So the duckling sat in a corner and felt very unhappy. Then he thought of the fresh air and the sunshine and was seized with such a strong desire to float upon the water that at last he could not help saying so to the hen.

"Why, what's the matter with you?" asked the hen. "This comes of being idle. You have nothing to do, and that's why you have all these ideas. Lay eggs or purr, and they'll go away."

"But it is so nice to float upon the water," said the duckling, "so nice to dive in headfirst and go right down to the bottom."

"Oh, most delightful, I am sure," said the hen. "You're mad, I think. Ask the cat. He's the wisest creature I know. If he likes floating on the water or diving in, I'll say no more. Ask our mistress, the old woman. There is no one in the whole world wiser than she. Do you think that *she* has any desire to float on the water and dive deep?"

"You don't understand me," said the duckling.

"If *we* don't understand you, I should like to know who does. You will never be wiser than the cat and the old woman, let alone myself. Don't make a fool of yourself, child, and thank goodness for all the kindness that has been shown to you. Have you not been invited into a warm room and into company from which you can learn something? But you're a wretch and conversation with you is anything but pleasant. You may take my word for it. I only mean it for your own good when I tell you unpleasant truths. It is only one's real friends who talk to one like that. See that you lay eggs and learn to purr or give out sparks."

"I think I will go out into the wide world," said the duckling.

"Do, by all means," said the hen.

So the duckling went. He floated upon the water, and dove in headfirst, but all the other animals looked down upon him because he was so ugly.

Then autumn came. The leaves of the forest grew yellow and brown. The wind caught hold of them and made them dance about, and the sky looked cold. The clouds hung heavy with hail and snow-flakes, and on the fence stood the raven, which cried, for sheer cold, "Ow! Ow!" Yes, the very thought of winter was enough to make one freeze. The poor duckling was miserable.

One evening the sun went down gloriously, and out from a large grove came a whole flock of lovely large birds. The duckling had never seen anything so beautiful. They were dazzlingly white with long, supple, graceful necks—they were swans. They uttered a strange cry, spread their splendid wings, and flew away from the cold fields toward warmer lands and open lakes. They rose so high that the ugly little duckling felt quite strange. He turned around in the water like a wheel, stretched his neck after them high in the air, and uttered such a loud and odd shriek that he was frightened at his own voice. Oh, he could not forget the beautiful birds, the happy birds, and as soon as he had lost sight of them altogether, he ducked right down to the bottom. When he came up again he was quite beside himself. He did not know the name of the birds, or where they were flying, yet he loved them as he had never loved anything before. This was not envy. How could the duckling presume to wish for such loveliness. He would have been only too glad if they had allowed him, a poor ugly creature, to go with them.

And the winter grew cold, so cold that the duckling had to keep swimming on the water to keep from freezing. But every night the area in which it swam became smaller and smaller. It froze so that the whole crust of ice crackled again and the duckling had to kick his legs continually so that the surface of the water would not freeze completely and close up. At last the poor duckling grew faint, lay quite still, and froze solid into the ice.

 65

Early the next morning a farmer came along. He saw the duckling and went out to him; then he broke the ice with his wooden shoe, and brought the bird home to his wife. There the bird revived.

The children wanted to play with him, but the duckling thought they were trying to hurt him. In fright he flew right into the milk can, and milk splashed all about the room. The woman shrieked and

struck out with her hands. Then the duckling flew into the butter tub, and down into the flour barrel and out again, by which time it was quite a sight. The woman shrieked and flung the fire irons at him. The children tumbled over each other's legs trying to catch the duckling, and they laughed and shrieked again. Fortunately, the door was open, and out rushed the duckling into the freshly fallen snow among the bushes, and there he lay, exhausted.

The poor duckling suffered terribly that hard winter. Then, one day, he was lying in the marsh among the tall grasses when the sun again began to shine warmly. The larks were singing. It was beautiful springtime.

A week later the duckling stretched out his wings. They flapped stronger than before and carried him easily into the air. Before he knew where he was, the duckling found himself in a large garden where apple trees were in full bloom, where the lilac flowers smelled so sweetly. They hung on long green branches right near the winding waterway. Oh, it was lovely here, so full of the freshness of spring. Then, from out of the thicket came three beautiful white swans. They made a rushing sound with their wings and floated upon the water. The duckling recognized the splendid creatures and was overcome by a strange feeling of sorrow.

"I will fly toward the royal birds. They will peck me to death because I, who am so ugly, dare to approach them, but it is all the same to me. Better to be slain by them than to be nipped by the ducks, pecked by the hens, kicked by the girl who looks after the poultry, and to be hungry and cold all winter."

So the duckling flew out into the water and swam toward the stately swans, who saw him and came darting toward him.

"Kill me and be done with me," cried the poor creature. He bowed his head toward the water to await death. But what did he see in the clear water? His own image. He was no longer a clumsy, dark gray bird. He was a swan. It doesn't matter a bit about being born in a duckyard when one has hatched from a swan's egg.

The large swans now swam around and around him. They stroked him with their beaks and were quite friendly.

Some little children came running into the garden. They threw corn and breadcrumbs on the water, and the smallest of them exclaimed, "There's a new one!" The other children also shouted, "Yes! A new one has come!" And they clapped their hands and danced about and ran to fetch their father and mother. Then bread and cakes were thrown into the water, and the largest child said, "The new one is the prettiest! It is so young and lovely." And the old swans bowed before it.

He felt so bashful that he stuck his head beneath his wings. He did not know what to do. He was almost too happy, but not a bit proud, for a good heart is never proud. He thought of how he had been persecuted and despised, yet now everyone said that he was the loveliest of lovely birds. And the lilacs bowed their branches down into the water toward him, and the sun shone so nice and warm, and then the young swan swelled out his plumage, raised his slim neck, and cried from the bottom of his heart, "I never dreamed of such happiness when I was an ugly duckling!"

The Princess
and the Pea

HERE was once a Prince who was determined to marry a Princess, but she had to be a *real* Princess. So he roamed the whole world over to find one, but there was always something wrong. He found plenty of princesses, but he could never make up his mind whether they were *real* princesses. There was always something that was not quite as he felt it ought to be. So home he came again, and was much distressed, for he absolutely longed for a real Princess.

One evening there was a terrible storm. It thundered and lightninged, the rain poured in torrents—it was positively dreadful. Then there came a knocking at the city gate. The old King went and opened it.

A Princess stood outside, but oh, what a fright she looked in the rain and wet weather. The water dripped down her hair and clothes, and ran into the tips of her shoes and out again at the heels. Yet she said she was a real Princess.

Indeed! We'll see about that soon enough, thought the old Queen. She said nothing, but went into her bedroom, took off all the bedding, and placed a pea at the bottom of the bed. Then she took twenty mattresses and laid them above the pea. Finally, on top of the mattresses, she piled twenty down quilts.

There the Princess was to sleep that night.

In the morning the Queen asked her how she had slept.

"Oh, horribly!" said the Princess. "I have scarcely had a wink of sleep all night. Heaven knows what there was in my bed! I have been lying on something hard, for my whole body is black-and-blue! It is perfectly frightful!"

So they could see at once that this was a real Princess, for she had felt the pea through twenty mattresses and twenty down quilts. No one but a real Princess could have had such delicate feeling as that.

Then the Prince married her, for now he was quite sure she was a real Princess, and the pea was preserved in the royal cabinet of curiosities, where it may still be seen, if no one has taken it away.

The
Little Mermaid

AR OUT at sea the water is as blue as the loveliest cornflower and as clear as the purest crystal. But it is very deep—deeper than any anchor has ever reached. Many church steeples would have to be piled one upon the other to reach from the bottom to the surface. Down there dwell the sea folk.

Now you must by no means imagine that there is nothing below the sea but bare white sand. No, indeed! The most wondrous trees and plants grow there. Their stalks and leaves are so supple that they wave to and fro at the slightest motion of the water. All the fish, small and great, glide through the branches just as the birds fly about the trees upon the earth. In the deepest spot of all stands the Sea King's palace. The walls are made of coral and the tall, pointed windows of the clearest amber, while the roof is made of mussel shells, which open and close according to the tide. And in each lies a glistening pearl, worthy of a queen's crown.

The Sea King had been a widower for many years, so his aged mother kept house for him. She was a wise woman and very proud of her noble birth, which entitled her to wear twelve oysters on her tail, while the other important folk were allowed to wear only six. Nevertheless she was very well respected, especially because of the loving care she took of the little sea princesses, her granddaughters.

They were six pretty children, but the youngest was the loveliest of them all. Her skin was as delicately tinted as a rose petal, and her eyes were as blue as the deepest sea, but, like her sisters, she had no feet and her body ended in a fish's tail.

The princesses played all day long in the great rooms of the palace, where living flowers grew upon the walls. When the large amber windows were opened the fishes would swim in, right up to the little princesses, eat out of their hands, and allow themselves to be patted.

Around the palace there was a large garden full of bright red and dark blue trees. The fruit shone like gold, and the flowers glowed like burning fire, as the stalks and leaves moved to and fro. The soil itself was the finest sand, but it was as blue as the flames of burning sulfur. A wondrous blue tint covered everything, and it was as if you were hovering high up in the air with sky above and below rather than standing at the bottom of the sea. When the winds were calm, the sun was visible, and it looked like a crimson flower with light streaming out.

Each of the little princesses had her own little garden where she could dig and plant as she pleased. One planted her flowers in the shape of a whale. Another preferred hers to look like a little mermaid. But the youngest planted hers in a circle to imitate the sun and would grow only flowers that shone red like the sun. She was a strange child, silent and thoughtful, and while her sisters were delighted to adorn their gardens with all the strangest things they could get from wrecked vessels, all that she would have, besides the rosy red flowers that resembled the sun, was a pretty statue of a handsome boy, carved from pure white marble, which had sunk to the bottom of the sea during a shipwreck. Next to this statue she planted a rosy red weeping willow. It grew splendidly and its fresh branches hung over the statue, nearly down to the sandy bottom where the shadows looked violet and danced to and fro like the branches. It seemed as if the top of the tree were at play with its roots, each trying to snatch a kiss.

The young princess's greatest joy was to hear about the world above the sea. She made her grandmother tell her all she knew about ships and towns, people and animals. What struck her as most wonderful was that the flowers of the earth had lovely fragrances, which they did not have at the bottom of the sea; and that the woods were green and that the fish among the branches could sing so loudly and beautifully that it was a joy to listen to them. (Her grandmother called the little birds "fish," so that her listeners would understand her, for they had never seen birds.)

"When you have reached your fifteenth year," said the grandmother, "you shall be allowed to rise up out of the sea and sit on the rocks in the moonlight. From there you can see the big ships sail by, and you'll be able to see woods and cities, too."

In the following year one of the sisters would be fifteen years old, but how about the others? Each was a year younger than the one before, so the youngest would have to wait five whole years before it would be her turn to rise from the bottom of the sea and see what the world was like. But each promised to tell the others what she had seen and what she had thought was most remarkable, for their grandmother did not tell them enough to satisfy their curiosity, and there were many things they wanted to know about.

But none of them longed as much for her turn as the youngest, who had the most time to wait and was so silent and thoughtful. Many a night she stood at the open window and looked up through the dark blue water where the fish dashed about with their fins and tails. She could see the moon and stars. Of course, they shone quite faintly, and yet they looked twice as large through the water as they looked from the land. When something like a dark cloud glided across, she knew that it was either a whale swimming overhead, or a ship with many people on board, who certainly never dreamed that a pretty little mermaid stood below and stretched her white arms up toward the keel of their vessel.

One day the eldest Princess turned fifteen and was allowed to rise

to the surface of the sea. When she came back she had hundreds of things to tell about, but the nicest of all, she said, was to lie in the moonlight on a sandbank in the calm sea, and to see near the shore the large town where the lights were twinkling, like hundreds of stars, to hear the music and the noise and bustle of carriages and people, to look at the many church steeples and spires, and to hear the bells ringing. And because she could not go ashore, she longed so for all these things.

Oh, how the youngest sister listened. And afterward, in the evening when she stood at the open window and looked up through the dark blue water, she thought of the great city with all its noise and bustle, and even imagined she heard the church bells ringing.

The next year the second sister was permitted to rise up through the water and swim where she pleased. She rose just as the sun was going down and she told her sisters that the sunset was the prettiest sight of all. The whole sky looked like gold, she said, and the beauty of the clouds was beyond description. Red and violet clouds had sailed right over her head, while a flock of wild swans had flown, like a long white veil, toward the setting sun. She also swam toward the sun, but it sank, and the rosy gleam left behind was soon swallowed up by the sea and the clouds.

A year after that the third sister swam up to the surface. She was the boldest of them all, so she swam up a broad river that emptied into the sea. She saw pretty green hills covered with vines and castles and country houses that peeked out from stately woods. She heard the birds singing, and the sun shone so brightly that she often had to duck down under the water to cool her burning face. In a little creek she came upon a group of human children. They were naked and splashing in the water. She wanted to play with them, but they ran away in terror and a little black beast ran over to her. It was a dog, but she had never seen a dog before. It barked at her so savagely that she was frightened and swam quickly back to the open sea. But she could never forget the lovely woods, the green hills, and the pretty

children who could swim in the water although they had no fish tails.

The fourth sister was not so bold. She remained out in the middle of the sea and said that was nicest of all; for you could see for miles and miles around, and the sky above looked like a large glass bell. She saw ships too, but far away, and they looked like sea gulls. The merry dolphins turned somersaults and the great whales squirted water up through their nostrils, so that it seemed as if hundreds of fountains were playing all around.

And now it was the turn of the fifth sister. Her birthday was in the winter, and therefore she saw what the others had not seen when they went up. The sea looked green and huge icebergs floated about; each looked like a pearl, she said, and yet was far larger than the church steeples that human beings built. They had the strangest shapes and glittered like diamonds. She had placed herself on one of the largest, and all the ships scudded past in terror while she sat there and let the wind flutter her long streaming hair. But toward evening the sky became overcast. There was thunder and lightning, and the dark sea lifted the large icebergs high up so that they shone in the glare of the lightning. All the ships lowered their sails. Distress and horror reigned, but the little mermaid sat calmly on her iceberg and watched the lightning as it zigzagged into the troubled sea.

The first time any of the sisters rose to the surface of the water she was enraptured with the new and beautiful things she saw, but afterward, when as grown-ups they could go above whenever they chose, they became quite indifferent to such trips. They longed for the deep water, and in about a month would say that it was nicest down below, for there one felt so thoroughly at home.

Very often in the evenings the five sisters would entwine their arms and rise in a row to the surface of the water. They had beautiful voices, sweeter than any human voice, and when a storm was brewing and they had reason to believe a ship might be lost, they would swim before the ship and sing sweetly of the joys to be found at the bottom of the sea, telling the sailors not to be afraid to come down.

But the sailors could not understand their words. They thought the sound was the howling of the storm, and they never did see any of the beautiful things below, for when a ship sank the whole crew drowned.

When her sisters rose arm in arm through the sea, the little sister would remain below alone looking up after them, and she felt like crying, but mermaids have no tears and so suffer all the more.

"Oh, if only I were fifteen!" she said. "I know that I shall love the world above and the people who live there."

And at last she *was* fifteen years old.

"Well, now at last we have *you* off our hands," said her grandmother with a smile.

"Come here and let me dress you like your sisters." And she placed a wreath of white lilies in her hair, but every petal was half a pearl, and the old lady commanded eight large oysters to cling to the Princess's tail to show her high rank.

"But they hurt me so!" said the little mermaid.

"Yes, but one must suffer a little for the sake of appearances."

Oh, how gladly the little mermaid would have torn off all this finery and put aside her wreath; the red flowers from her garden suited her much better; but she dared not. "Farewell!" she said and rose, light and bright as a bubble, up to the surface of the water.

The sun had just sunk as she raised her head above the sea, but the clouds were still pink and gold, and in the midst of the pale sky sparkled the evening star, so clear and lovely. The air was mild and cool, and the sea as still as a mirror.

A large black ship with three masts was becalmed on the sea. Only a single sail was up, for no wind stirred, and the sailors sat idly on the masts and rigging, playing music and singing. As the evening darkened hundreds of colorful lamps were lit. The little mermaid swam close to the cabin window, and every time the waves lifted her she would peek in through the panes and could see many finely dressed people. The handsomest was certainly the young Prince, who had

large black eyes. He could not be more than sixteen years old, and it was *his* birthday. That was the reason for all this merriment. The sailors danced on the deck, and when the young Prince stepped up, more than a hundred rockets rose into the air. They shone as bright as day, so that the little mermaid was frightened and dived beneath the water. But she soon popped her head up again and then it seemed as if all the stars of heaven were falling down upon her. Never had she seen such fireworks; large suns spun around and around, throwing out sparks; splendid fiery fishes dashed about in the blue air, and everything was reflected in the clear, calm sea. On the ship itself it was so light that you could clearly see every rope and spar and every person. And oh, how handsome the young Prince looked as he greeted people and laughed and smiled while the music resounded through the lovely night.

It grew late, but the little mermaid could not take her eyes from the ship and the handsome Prince. The many-colored lanterns were put out. No more rockets rose into the air, and no more cannons were fired. But from deep down in the sea there came a murmuring and a roaring. Still she sat upon the water, rocking up and down with the waves so she could look into the cabin. But now the ship took a swifter course. One sail after another was lowered. The waves rolled higher and lightning came from far away.

A frightful storm was coming; that was why the sailors pulled in the sails. The huge ship pitched to and fro as it flew across the raging ocean. The waves rose like great black mountains. It seemed as if they would roll right over the masts, but the ship dove like a swan and then rose again on the towering waves. Although the little mermaid thought this was great fun, the sailors certainly didn't. The ship strained and cracked, the thick planks bent under the repeated pounding of the sea. Then the mast snapped in the middle, and the ship rolled over on her side while the water rushed in. Now the little mermaid realized that they were in grave danger, and she herself had to beware of the beams and wreckage of the ship.

 82

For a moment it was so dark that she could see nothing at all, but then a flash of lightning illuminated the ship and she saw everybody tumbling about. She looked especially for the young Prince. As the ship fell to pieces she saw him sink into the deep sea. She was quite pleased, for now he would come down to her. Then it occurred to her that human beings cannot live under the water and that he would be dead by the time he reached her father's palace. Die he must not, oh no! So she swam among the beams and planks that tossed on the sea, quite forgetting that they might crush her. Then she dove deep into the water and, rising again on the waves, managed at last to reach the young Prince, who by now was scarcely able to swim in the raging sea. His arms and legs began to fail him, his beautiful eyes were closed. He would surely have died if the little mermaid had not

 83

come to his assistance. She held his head above the water and then let the waves carry them along.

When morning dawned the storm had passed, but not a fragment of the ship was to be seen. The sun rose red and beaming from the water. The Prince's cheeks were no longer deathly pale, but his eyes remained closed. The mermaid kissed his high handsome forehead and stroked his wet hair. He looked just like the marble statue down in her little garden. She kissed him again and wished that he might live.

And now, before her, she saw the mainland, with lofty blue mountains on which the snow shone as if great flocks of white swans had gathered. Near the shore were lovely green forests and in front stood a church or convent, she did not exactly know what—but it was a large building of some sort. Lemon and orange trees grew in the garden, and in front of the gate stood tall palm trees. The sea formed a little bay here; it was quite calm but very deep, right up to the cliff where the sea had washed up the fine white sand. There she swam with the handsome Prince and laid him on the sand in the warm sunshine. She took great care to place his head higher than his body.

The bells in the large white building started ringing, and a group of girls came walking through the garden. The little mermaid swam farther out behind some high rocks that rose out of the water; she covered herself with sea foam so no one could see her face. There she watched to see who would come to the aid of the poor Prince.

It was not long before a young girl came along. She was quite frightened when she saw him, but only for a moment. Then she brought over a number of people, and the mermaid saw that the Prince came to life again, and smiled at those around him. But he did not send a smile to her, for, of course, he did not know that she had saved him. She felt so unhappy that when he was carried away into the large building she dived down under the water full of sorrow and returned to her father's palace.

The little mermaid had always been silent and thoughtful, but after

this she became even more so. Her sisters asked her what she had seen when she went above for the first time, but she would tell them nothing.

Many a morning and many an evening she rose to the spot where she had last seen the Prince. She saw how the fruits of the garden ripened and were plucked. She saw how the snow melted on the high mountains, but she did not see the Prince, and every time she returned home more and more sorrowful. Her only consolation was to sit in her little garden and fling her arms around the pretty marble statue that was so like the Prince. But she did not tend to her flowers at all. They grew as if in a wilderness all over the paths and entwined their long stalks and leaves among the branches of the trees until it was quite gloomy beneath their shade.

At last the little mermaid could endure her sorrow no longer and told her story to one of her sisters, who told all the others. Then it reached the ears of two other mermaids, who told it to nobody but their closest friends. One of these happened to know all about the Prince. She, too, had seen the merrymaking on board the ship and knew where the Prince came from and where his kingdom was.

"Come, little sister!" said the other princesses, and with their arms around each other's shoulders, they rose in a long row out of the sea near the place where they knew the Prince's palace stood. It was built of a light yellow glistening stone, with broad marble staircases, one of which reached straight down to the sea. Gorgeous gilded cupolas rose above the roof, and between the columns that surrounded the whole building stood lifelike marble statues. Through the high windows they could see into magnificent rooms hung with costly silk curtains and tapestries, and all the walls were adorned with large, beautiful pictures. In the midst of the main room splashed a large fountain, with water rising high into the air toward the glass cupola. Through the cupola the sun shone down upon the water and the beautiful plants growing there.

So now the little mermaid knew where the Prince lived, and many

an evening and many a night she rose up through the water. She swam much nearer to the land than any of her sisters had dared to do. She even went up the narrow canal, under the marble balcony that cast a long shadow across the water. Here she would sit and gaze at the young Prince, who thought he was quite alone in the bright moonlight.

Many evenings she saw him sail in his splendid boat with banners waving and music playing. She would peek from among the green rushes, and when the wind played with her long silvery white veil and people caught sight of it, they thought it was a swan spreading its wings.

Many nights, too, when the fishermen were spreading their nets by torchlight, she heard them speaking of the young Prince and praising him so highly that she was more glad than ever that she had saved his life when he was tossed about by the waves. And she remembered how his head had rested against her, and how she had kissed him. But since he knew nothing of all this, he could not even dream about her.

So she grew to love people more and more, and to long more and more to be among them. Their world seemed so much grander than her own; why, they could fly across the sea in ships, ascend the lofty mountains high above the clouds, and the land they called their own extended farther than her eye could reach.

There was much she would have liked to know, but her sisters were not able to answer her questions. She therefore asked her grandmother, who knew all about the upper world.

"If men do not get drowned," asked the little mermaid, "can they live forever? Don't they die as we do down here in the sea?"

"Yes," said the old lady, "they too must die. And indeed their life is shorter than ours. We can live to be three hundred years old, but when at last we cease to be, we become mere foam upon the water. Our souls are not immortal; we never enter upon a new life. We are like the green rushes: once they are cut down, they cannot grow

 87

again. Human beings, on the other hand, have souls that live forever—even after the body has been buried in the earth—and their souls rise up through the clear air to the shining stars. Just as we rise out of the sea up to the lands above, so their souls mount to beautiful unknown regions of which we shall never catch a glimpse.''

''Why have we not immortal souls?'' asked the little mermaid sorrowfully. ''I would give all the hundreds of years I may have to live if I could be a human being for only a single day so that I might hope to live in the world above the sky.''

''You must not bother your head about that,'' said her old grandmother. ''We have a much better and happier lot than the people above.''

''So I shall die and drift away like foam upon the sea, never again to hear the music of the waves, or to see the pretty flowers and the red sun. Can I do nothing at all to win an immortal soul?''

''No,'' said her old grandmother. ''Only if a human being grew to love you so dearly that you meant more to him than father or mother, if he loved you with all his heart and soul, and let the priest lay his right hand in yours and vowed to be faithful to you here and in all eternity, then his soul would flow over to your body and you would have a share in the bliss that comes to human beings. He would have given you a soul without giving up his own. But that can never be. The very thing that is so pretty in the sea, here, your fish's tail, is considered hideous on earth because they know no better. Up there one must have a couple of awkward things called legs to be thought handsome.''

Then the little mermaid sighed and looked sorrowfully down at her fish's tail.

''Let us be content with our lot,'' said her grandmother, ''and hop and skip about to our hearts' content in the three hundred years we have to live in. Upon my word we have a nice long time of it. We'll have a court ball this very evening!''

It was indeed a gorgeous sight, such as is never seen on earth. The

walls and ceiling of the vast dancing hall were of glass, thick but clear. Many hundreds of huge shells, rosy red and grassy green, which hung in rows on each side, were full of blue blazing flames that lit up the whole room and shone right through the walls, so the sea around was also bright. Countless fish, both small and great, came swimming past the glass walls. Some of their scales shone purple and red, while others sparkled like gold and silver.

Through the great ballroom flowed a wide stream, and on this the mermen and the mermaids danced to their own pretty songs. Such lovely voices were unknown on earth.

The little mermaid sang the sweetest of them all and they applauded her loudly. For a moment her heart was glad, for she knew that she had the loveliest voice of all creatures on the earth or in the sea. But soon her thoughts turned once more to the world above her. She could forget neither the handsome Prince nor her sorrow at not possessing, like him, an immortal soul. So she soon sneaked away from her father's palace, with its mirth and melody, and sat sorrowfully in her little garden.

Here she heard a bugle sounding down through the water and she thought, Now I know *he* is sailing up above there—he whom I love more than my father or mother and in whose hands I would willingly entrust my life's happiness. I will venture everything to win him and an immortal soul! While my sisters are dancing in my father's palace, I will go to the sea witch. I have always been afraid of her, but perhaps she can advise me and help me."

So the little mermaid left her own part of the sea and swam toward a raging whirpool behind which the sea witch lived. She had never gone that way before. No flowers nor sea grasses grew there. Only the bare gray sandy bottom stretched out toward the whirlpool where the water eddied around and around, dragging everything it caught into the deep. She had to go right through these buffeting whirlpools to reach the sea witch's domain, and here, for quite a distance, she had to pass across hot bubbling mud. Beyond this stood

the sea witch's house in the midst of a strange wood. All the trees and bushes were polypi—half animal, half vegetable—they looked like hundred-headed serpents growing out of the ground. Their branches were long slimy arms, with fingers like snakes, and they twisted and twirled from their roots to the outermost tips of their branches. Anything that they could grab hold of they wound themselves around and never let go.

The little mermaid was terrified and remained standing there, her heart thumping with fear. She almost turned back, but then she thought of the Prince and of the human soul, and her courage returned. She bound her long flowing hair close to her head, so that the polypi could not seize it. Then she crossed both hands over her chest, and darted through the water as only fish can, right between the hideous polypi, which stretched out their long supple arms and fingers after her. She saw that nearly every one of them still gripped something in its hundreds of little fingers, which were as strong as iron bands. The white skeletons of human beings who had perished in the sea peeked out from the arms of the polypi. They held fast to ship's rudders and beams, too. She saw the skeletons of land animals and even a little mermaid whom they had caught and crushed to death; to her that was the most terrible sight of all.

And now she came to a great slimy open swamp in the wood, where large fat watersnakes were wallowing and showing their ugly whitish-yellow bellies. In the midst of this swamp a house had been built from the bones of shipwrecked men. And here sat the sea witch, letting a toad eat from her hand. She called the hideous fat watersnakes her chicks and let them creep all over her large spongy body.

"I know what you want," said the sea witch. "You're a fool for your pains. Nevertheless you shall have your own way, for you will get into trouble, my pretty Princess. You want to be rid of your fish's tail, eh? And to have a couple of stumps to walk about on, as people have, so the young Prince will fall in love with you, and you may get him and an immortal soul in the bargain!"

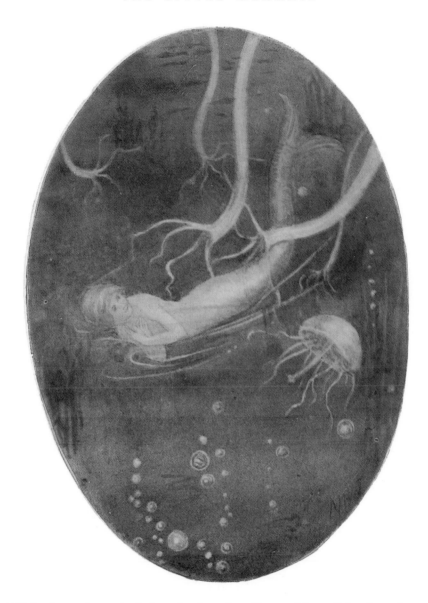

With that, the witch laughed so loudly and horribly that the toad and the snakes fell to the ground, where they lay wriggling.

"You have come in the very nick of time," said the witch. "If you had put it off until tomorrow, at sunrise, I should not have been able

 91

to help you for another year. I will brew you a potion, and you must swim to land, sit on the shore, and drink it all before sunrise. Then your tail will split and shrivel up into what people call nice legs. But it will hurt, mind you, for it will be like a sharp sword piercing you. All who see you will say that you are the loveliest mortal they ever saw. You will keep your elegant floating walk—no dancing girl will be able to move so lightly as you—but every stride you take will feel as if you are treading on sharp knives. If you still choose to suffer all this, I have the power to help you."

"I do," said the little mermaid in a trembling voice. She thought of the Prince and of winning an immortal soul.

"But remember," said the witch, "once you have a human form you can never become a mermaid again. You will never be able to dive down through the water to your sisters or return to your father's palace. And if you should fail to win the Prince's love so that, for your sake, he forgets father and mother and loves you with all his soul, and lets the priest join your hands and make you man and wife, you will not obtain an immortal soul! The very first morning after he has married another your heart will break and you will become mere foam upon the waves!"

"Be it so," said the little mermaid, but she was as pale as death.

"But you must pay me, too," said the witch, "and it will not be a small thing either that I demand. You have the loveliest voice of all things here at the bottom of the sea, and you think you will enchant him with that, I know. But you will not, for you must give that voice to me. I choose to have your best possession in return for my precious potion, for I must mix my own blood into it so that the potion will be as sharp as a two-edged sword."

"But if you take my voice," asked the little mermaid, "what will I have left?"

"Your lovely form," said the witch, "your graceful movement and your expressive eyes—you can win a man's heart with them, I suppose. Well, have you lost courage, eh? Put out your little tongue

and I will cut it off in payment, and you shall have the precious potion!"

"Be it so, then!" said the little mermaid, and the witch put her kettle on the fire to brew the magic potion. "Cleanliness is a virtue," said she, and she scoured out the cauldron with the snakes she had tied into a knot for the purpose. Then she pricked herself and let her black blood drip down into the cauldron. The steam that rose from it took the strangest shapes, so that looking at them caused anguish and terror. Every moment the witch added something else to the cauldron. When the concoction began to boil, it made a noise like a weeping crocodile. But when the drink was finally ready, it looked like the clearest water.

"Here you are," said the witch, and cut out the tongue of the little mermaid, so that she could now neither sing nor talk.

"If the polypi grip you as you go back through the wood," said the witch, "just throw a single drop of this potion over them, and their arms and fingers will burst into a thousand pieces." But the little mermaid had no need to do this. The polypi shrank from her in terror when they saw the potion, which shone in her hand like a dazzling star. So she quickly she got through the wood, the swamp, and the raging whirlpool.

She could see her father's palace; the lights were off in the long dancing hall—all within were doubtless asleep—but she dared not visit them now that she could not speak and was about to go away from them forever. Her heart felt as if it must burst with sorrow. She stole into the garden, plucked a flower from each of her sisters' flower beds, threw a thousand kisses toward the palace, and rose up through the dark blue waters.

The sun was not yet up when she saw the Prince's palace and reached the splendid marble staircase. The moon was shining bright and beautiful. The little mermaid drank the sharp burning potion, and it was as though a two-edged sword pierced right through her body. She moaned with agony and lay there as if dead.

When the sun rose over the sea she woke and felt a sharp pang. But right in front of her stood the handsome young Prince. He fixed his coal-black eyes upon her so intently that she cast her own eyes down and saw that her fish tail had disappeared, and that she had the prettiest little white legs. But she was quite naked, so she wrapped herself in her long, thick hair. The Prince asked who she was and how she had come there, but she could only look at him shyly and sadly with her dark blue eyes, for she could not speak. Then he took her by the hand and led her into the palace. Every step she took felt, as the witch had predicted, as if she were treading on points of needles or sharp knives. But she willingly bore the pain, and holding the Prince's hand she mounted the staircase as light as a bubble, so that he and all who saw her were amazed at her light and graceful movements.

Soon she was dressed in the most costly garments, all silk and muslin. No one in the whole palace was so lovely, but she could neither sing nor speak. Lovely entertainers, dressed in silk and gold, came and sang to the Prince and his royal parents. One of them sang more sweetly than the rest, and the Prince clapped his hands and smiled at her. This troubled the little mermaid. She knew that she herself had sung far more sweetly, and she thought, Oh, that he might know that for the sake of being near him I have given away my voice forever!

Then the entertainers danced some light and graceful measures to the loveliest music. At this the little mermaid lifted her white arms, raised herself on the tips of her toes, and floated lightly across the floor as none had ever done before. Every movement made her beauty more apparent and her eyes spoke more deeply to the heart than did any of the songs of the others.

Everybody was enchanted with her, especially the Prince, who called her his little foundling, and she danced more and more, although every time her feet touched the floor it was as if she stepped on a sharp knife. The Prince declared that she should always be by his side.

He had the seamstress make a man's riding outfit so that she could accompany him on horseback. They rode together through the fragrant woods, where green branches touched their shoulders and little birds sang among the fresh green leaves. With the Prince she climbed up the high mountains, and although her tender feet bled so others saw it, she only laughed at the suffering and followed him until they saw the clouds sailing below them like flocks of birds flying to a foreign land.

At night, in the Prince's palace, while others slept she would go out on the broad marble steps, for it cooled her burning feet to stand in the cold seawater. Then she thought of the friends she had left in the depths below.

One night her sisters rose up arm in arm and sang sorrowfully as they swam in the water. She nodded to them, and they recognized her and told her how miserable she had made them all by going away.

After that, they visited her every night, and once she saw, a long way off, her grandmother, who had not come up above the sea for many years, and the Sea King with his crown upon his head. They stretched out their hands toward her, but dared not come as close to land as her sisters did.

Every day she became dearer to the Prince, who loved her as one might love a dear, good child. But to make her his queen never entered his mind. Yet his wife she must become, or she would never obtain an immortal soul, but would melt to foam on the morning of his wedding to another.

"Do you love me most of all?" the eyes of the little mermaid seemed to ask when he took her in his arms and kissed her fair brow.

"Yes, you are dearest of all to me," said the Prince, "for you have the best heart. You are the most devoted to me, and you are just like a lovely maiden I once saw but shall never see again. I was on a ship

that was wrecked, and the waves cast me ashore near a convent, where many young girls were studying. The youngest found me on the shore and saved my life. I saw her only twice. She is the only one I could love in this world. But you are so like her, you almost drive her image from my soul. She belongs to the convent, and my good fortune has sent you to me instead of her, and we will never part.''

Alas! he does not know that it was I who saved his life, thought the little mermaid. I bore him right over the sea to the wood where the convent stands. I sat beneath the foam and looked to see if anyone would come. I saw the pretty girl whom he loves better than he does me. And the mermaid sighed deeply but she could not cry. He says the girl belongs to that convent, that she will never come out into the world, and that they will never meet again. I am with him, I see him every day, I will cherish and love him.

But now came talk that the Prince was to marry the lovely daughter of the neighboring king, and that was why he now set about fitting out a splendid ship. ''The Prince is traveling to see the land of the neighboring king,'' people said, but everyone knew it was really to see the neighboring king's daughter that he went off with such a grand entourage.

The little mermaid shook her head and smiled. She knew the Prince's thoughts better than all the others did. ''I must travel,'' he had said to her. ''I must see this beautiful Princess—my parents insist on it—but they shall not force me to bring her home as my bride. I cannot love her. She is not like the lovely girl in the convent whom you are like. If I ever choose a bride, it would be you, my mute foundling with the speaking eyes!'' And he kissed her rosy mouth, played with her long hair, and laid his head close to her heart while she dreamed of human bliss and an immortal soul.

''Surely you are not frightened by the sea, my sweet child?'' he said as they stood on the fine ship that was to carry him to the land of the neighboring king. And he talked to her of storm and calm, of the strange fish of the deep, and what the divers see down there, and she

smiled, for she knew better than anyone else about life at the bottom of the sea.

On the moonlit nights, when everyone on board was asleep except the captain at the helm, she sat at the side of the ship and looked down through the clear water and seemed to see her father's palace. High above it stood her grandmother with her silver crown on her head, staring up at the ship's keel through the contrary currents. Then her sisters came up to the surface of the water and gazed sadly at her and wrung their white hands. She beckoned to them, smiled, and would have told them that she was well and happy, but the cabin boy approached at that moment and her sisters dived beneath the waves, so that she half believed the white things she had seen were only foam upon the waters.

The next morning the ship sailed into the port of the neighboring king's splendid capital. The church bells were ringing. Trumpets sounded from the tops of the high towers. Soldiers stood at attention with waving banners and flashing spears.

Every day now brought a lavish feast or entertainment. Balls and parties followed in rapid succession, but the Princess was not yet there, for she had been brought up in a convent far away, they said, where she had learned all the royal virtues.

At last she arrived. Full of eagerness, the little mermaid stood there waiting to see her. She had to admit that she had never seen a more beautiful face. The Princess's skin was transparently fine, and from behind the long dark lashes sparkled dark blue, faithful eyes.

"It is you!" cried the Prince, "you who saved me when I lay like a corpse on the seashore!" And he embraced the blushing Princess. "Oh, I am so happy, I don't know what to do," he said to the little mermaid. "The very best I dared to hope has come to pass. You, too, will rejoice at my good fortune, for you love me more than all of them!" And the little mermaid kissed his hand, but she felt already that her heart would break. Yes, his bridal morning would mean death to her, and she would be changed forever into sea foam.

All the bells were ringing, and heralds rode through the streets to proclaim the marriage of the Prince and Princess.

Perfumed oil burned in precious silver lamps upon the altar. The priests swung their incense burners, and the bride and bridegroom held hands and received the bishop's blessing. The little mermaid, dressed in cloth of gold, stood there and held up the bride's train, but her ears did not hear the festive music, nor did her eyes see the sacred ceremony. She thought of her night of death, of all that she had lost in this world.

That same evening the bride and bridegroom went aboard the ship. Cannons roared and flags waved, and on the deck was placed a royal bridal tent of gold and purple.

The sails swelled out in the breeze, and the ship glided lightly over the ocean. When it grew dark, colored lamps were lit, and the sailors danced merrily on the deck. The little mermaid could not help thinking of the first time she had risen above the sea and seen the same gaiety and splendor. She whirled round and round in the dance, skimming along as the swallow skims when it is pursued. Everyone applauded her, for never before had she danced so beautifully. There was a piercing as of sharp knives in her feet, but she paid no attention; the anguish of her heart was far more piercing. She knew this was the last evening she would ever be able to see the Prince, for whom she had forsaken relatives and home, sacrificed her lovely voice, and suffered endless tortures day by day, without his even dreaming of it. It was the last night on which she was to breathe the same air as he, to look upon the deep sea and the star-lit sky. An eternal night, without a thought, or a dream, awaited her—for she had no soul and could not win one.

All was joy and gaiety on board the ship until long past midnight. And all the time she laughed and danced with the thought of death in her heart. The Prince kissed his lovely bride and she stroked his black hair, and arm in arm they went to rest in their splendid tent.

It grew dark and all was still on board. Only the ship's captain

stood there at the helm. The little mermaid leaned her white arms on the railing and looked toward the east for the rosy dawn. The first sunbeam, she knew, would kill her. Then she saw her sisters rise up from the sea, and they were as pale as she. Their long fair hair no longer streamed in the breeze. It had all been cut off.

"We have given it to the witch to secure help so that you will not die tonight! She has given us this knife. Look how sharp it is! Before the sun rises you must plunge it into the Prince's heart, and then, when his warm blood sprinkles your legs, they will again close up into a fish's tail, and you will once more be a mermaid, and may sink through the water to us, and live your three hundred years before you turn into sea foam. Hurry! Either he or you must die before sunrise. Our grandmother has sorrowed so that her hair has fallen out, as ours has fallen off beneath the witch's shears. Kill the Prince, and come back to us! Hurry! Don't you see the red streaks there in the sky? A few more minutes and the sun will rise and you will die." And they sighed deeply and sank beneath the waves.

The little mermaid drew aside the purple curtains from the tent and saw the beautiful bride asleep with her head on the Prince's breast. She bent down and kissed his fair forehead, then she looked up at the sky where the red dawn grew brighter and brighter. Then she stared at the sharp knife, and again turned her eyes to the Prince, who, in his dreams, called his bride by name; she alone was in his thoughts.

The knife quivered in the mermaid's hand. Should she strike? Another moment and she threw it far away in the waves. The water shone red where the knife fell, as if drops of blood gurgled up from the waves. Once again she gazed with aching eyes at the Prince, then she plunged from the ship into the sea, and felt her body dissolving into foam.

And now the sun rose out of the sea. Its rays fell with gentle warmth upon the cold sea foam, and the little mermaid did not feel the pangs

of death. She saw the bright sun, and above her floated hundreds of beautiful transparent shapes. She could still catch a glimpse of the white sails of the ship and of the red clouds in the sky. The voice of the shapes was all melody, but so ethereal that no human ear could hear it, just as no human eye could see them. They had no wings, but their very lightness held them in the air. The little mermaid saw that she now had a transparent body like theirs, and it rose higher and higher from the foam.

"To whom have I come?" she cried and her voice sounded like the voices of the other beings, so delicate that no earthly music could equal it.

"To the daughters of the air," they answered.

"A mermaid has no immortal soul, and can never have one unless she wins the love of a human being. Her eternal existence depends upon a power beyond her. The daughters of the air in the same way have no immortal soul, but they can get one by their good deeds. We fly to the hot countries, where the sultry air carries disease and death to children. We spread the fragrance of flowers through the air to heal and refresh the sufferers. When for three hundred years we have tried to do all the good in our power, we obtain an immortal soul and share the eternal destinies of the human race. You, poor little mermaid, have tried to do good with your whole heart. Like us, you have suffered and endured, and raised yourself into a spirit of the air. Now, therefore, you can win for yourself an immortal soul after three hundred years of good deeds."

And the little mermaid raised her bright arms toward the sun, and for the first time felt tears in her eyes.

There was activity on board the ship again. She saw the Prince and his beautiful bride looking for her, and then gazing sadly down at the bubbling foam, as if they knew she had plunged into the waves. Unseen by either of them, she kissed the bride's forehead, smiled upon the Prince, and rose with the other children of the air up to the rosy clouds that were sailing through the sky.

"For three hundred years we shall float and float until we glide right into the immortal kingdom," said a daughter of the air.

"Yes, and we may get there still sooner," whispered another. "Unseen we enter the houses where there are human children, and every day that we find a good child who gladdens his or her parents' hearts, and deserves their love, our time of trial is shortened. The child does not know when we fly through the room, but when we can smile with joy over it a whole year is taken from the three hundred. But whenever we see a disobedient and ill-behaved child we shed tears of sorrow, and every tear adds an extra day to our time of trial."

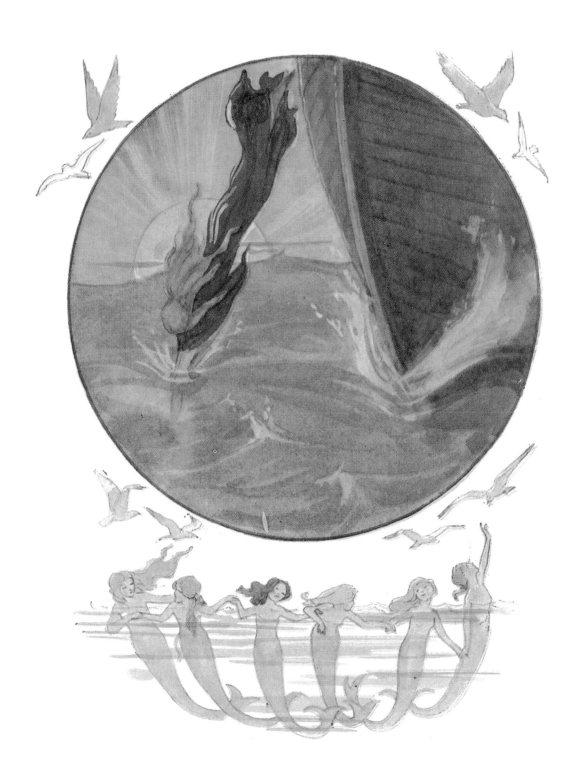